CASSIE MINT

Sweet Tooth

BLACK CHERRY

P U B L I S H I N G

First published by Black Cherry Publishing 2022

Copyright © 2022 by Cassie Mint

First edition

ISBN: 978-1-914242-93-9

This book was professionally typeset on Reedsy.
Find out more at reedsy.com

Contents

Keep in touch with Cassie!

Want to stay up to date with new releases, sales, and more instalove goodness?

Sign up for Cassie's newsletter!

One

Julian

Y ou know what it takes to be a lawyer? A *great* one?
People think you need to argue well and bullshit even
better–and sure, those are important skills, but they're
not the magic ingredient. They won't get you a corner office
on the top floor.

People think of sharp suits and buffed leather shoes and
expensive haircuts, like you can win over a judge or jury simply
by looking the part. And okay, there's some truth to that too.

People think lawyers need to be assholes. That you can't give
a shit about the world. I say that's optional, but fine.

And people say you need to hold your liquor and schmooze
your way around the city, taking cards and remembering names.
Again, a kernel of truth, but that's not all.

The one skill you *really* need, that you won't last a day of law
school without, let alone the job? You've got to thrive under
pressure. You've got to see the work piling up and the deadlines

coming in fast and the competition probing at your soft spots, and instead of panicking or daydreaming about buying a farm in the country or some shit, you've got to *smile.* Like you're on top of the fucking world.

It's a challenge, that's all. A chance to sharpen those teeth. A chance to show these other assholes that you're not to be trifled with.

And hardest of all, you've got to *mean* it. Can't fake low blood pressure–not for long. Either you're up to this, or you're not.

Anyway. I'm the biggest shark on the thirty-third floor, and the only way up from here is to make partner. I've got the big corner office and my own assistant. He screens my calls and waters my plants and makes me coffee from the machine the bosses gave me last year.

Vance and Irving both came down from the top floor and watched me drink the first cup, beaming with pride like they were watching their kid take his first driving lesson. It was weird, but I played along, toasting them both with a dark roast. Anything for the job. Thanks, dads!

I've come this far. Partner is so close I can *taste* it. I'm not going to fuck everything up now.

* * *

"Rodriguez."

Vance corners me in the elevator first thing on Monday morning, mopping the top of his bald head with a silk handkerchief as the doors slide shut behind him. It's just the two of us and a delivery guy—some acne-spotted kid drowning in his uniform and clutching a stack of parcels to his skinny chest.

I check my watch discreetly. I'm early. This is fine.

Julian

"Morning, sir." I shift over, conceding a few inches of space. I give him the perfect amount–enough to show deference, but not enough to imply fear. I've been playing this game for almost a decade now, and I'm good at it. The best. "You play golf on the weekend?"

Vance *always* plays golf on the weekend. Those clubs are an extension of his gnarled hands.

"A few rounds, a few rounds..." The boss is distracted. He scrubs the handkerchief over his face, then clears his throat, shooting me a glance. "Are you busy, Rodriguez? Can you spare a few minutes on the top floor?"

This is a trick question. If I say I'm busy, I'm blowing off the boss. Obvious error. If I say I'm free, he'll think I'm not pulling my weight.

"I can move some things around," I tell him smoothly. "I'll make it up over lunch. What do you need?"

Bingo. Vance shoots me a grateful smile, tucking his handkerchief away.

Don't let his sweet-old-man act fool you. Irving and Vance both shuffle around this building like friendly grandpas, practically digging in their pockets for boiled sweets for the interns, but they built this firm from nothing, and they have the hunting trophies to prove it.

Figuratively speaking. Hunting is too boisterous for these two, especially at their age. All I'm saying is they've buried a lot of competitors in their day. Their desk chairs could be piles of bones.

"We'll speak upstairs."

Okay. That's fine. Most information that passes through this building is sensitive in some way, and we don't want the delivery guy getting an earful. He's already tense enough, the

3

tips of his big ears turning pink.

It's like he can sense he's stepped into the tiger cage. Smart kid.

The elevator climbs quickly, cold seeping through the external glass wall. The city skyline is dark against the sunrise, and thousands of lights are still on, winking gold from the high rises.

We let the delivery kid out on floor twenty seven.

"It's nothing," Vance says a moment later, even though I didn't ask. The elevator floor purrs beneath our feet. "Nothing to worry about, Julian."

Nothing to worry about?

And he's calling me by my first name?

Well, shit.

* * *

I get a two minute elevator ride and a brisk walk down a carpeted corridor before we push into one of the top floor meeting rooms. That's my shot to prepare. In that time, I've run through every case I've had for the last six months. Every interaction with a major player in the city.

There's nothing. I'm sure of it. I win my cases, and I bring this firm big money. I don't screw around with interns, and I pass on tips to the higher-ups. So why the hell have they pulled me up here on a Monday morning?

Nothing to worry about, Vance said. People don't say shit like that when they've got good news. That's what you say when you're trying to soften a blow. He leads me into the meeting room now, and Irving stands to greet us at the conference table. The sky is getting lighter behind him.

Two old lawyers. Vance is stocky; Irving is gaunt. Vance is bald; Irving has a bristly mustache. Vance favors pinstripes, and Irving likes pale pink pocket squares.

That's it. Those are all the differences. But one big thing they have in common is the insistence on using a meeting room when they're both required to be present. God forbid one of them attend the other's office. It'd mean conceding ground.

So here we are, on neutral territory. I resist the urge to fiddle with my cuffs.

"What can I do for you, sirs?"

They like that. Vance and Irving share a conspiratorial smile, playing the misty-eyed fathers routine again. Give me a break.

None of us would be here if we weren't made of pure ambition.

They sit, so I sit. There's a jug of water, so I pour three glasses. Irving is slightly closer so I pass him a glass first, and Vance's eye twitches in response.

Clink. I set his down. He'll get over it.

Glasses delivered, I settle in my chair. From the outside, I know exactly how I look: relaxed. Confident. Pristinely dressed, with a charcoal waistcoat and burgundy tie. Bearded, yes, but it's a *trimmed* beard. No scruff in sight.

Inside, though, there's acid eating through my guts. I like pressure, yes, but not walking into a trap. I worked too hard in this firm. I don't want any damn curve balls, that's for sure.

"Julian." Vance says my name fondly. Irving bristles, annoyed that the other man's taken the lead. "You've worked here for how long now—six years?"

"Eight," I say. He knows that, the asshole, he's just trying to worry me. Trying to make me feel unnoticed and disposable to them. But two can play at that game, and I lean back with a broad smile. "Yes, it's rather a long time, isn't it?"

Read: I can walk any time I like, you wrinkly fuckers, and I'll take your bottom line with me. Don't try this shit on me.

Irving clears his throat. "Quite."

Vance's voice is cooler when he speaks again, but that's fine. Better that he's wary of me than taking me for granted. "You're due to make partner, of course. There's no one better for the honor. No lawyer more deserving in the building."

...Here we go.

"But?" I drum my fingers against the table, impatient for the punchline. This is not a celebratory conversation. This is a shakedown. "What's the catch, sir?"

Out comes the handkerchief again. He swabs at his forehead, then gestures for Irving to take over, face flushed.

The other man looks sour, but he picks up the thread. I'll remember that in the future–that Irving had the backbone, not Vance. "But we have a problem we'd like you to solve for us first. Or rather... there is a task. Of an unusual nature."

I roll my stiff neck, breathing in through my nose. An unusual task? That could be anything, and I won't react until I hear what it is.

Finally realizing that I don't plan on speaking just yet, Irving pushes on. He flattens his palms on the conference table, and his next words are stilted. Rehearsed. "Do you know the Briggs family, Julian?"

Obviously. "They're our biggest clients." They're old money–the kind of family that comes with an investment empire attached. Trust funds and charities. Prenups and divorce settlements. So many properties, they've probably forgotten about a few. The Briggs family could keep dozens of lawyers busy year-round.

6

Irving nods and pushes on, still talking like he's reading off a note card. "Well, the Briggs family has asked us for a small favor. Their business is very important to us, of course."

"Naturally."

"And this favor requires someone we trust."

So whatever it is, the bosses can't—or won't—do it. But they won't ship it out to just anyone, either, not when the stakes are so high.

I'm so fucking close to making partner. Once I land that promotion, I'll be on the fast track. More money, bigger clients, freedom from *this* type of bullshit. Then one day, once I've milked Irving & Vance for all the company's worth, I'll start my own firm—and I'll do it with a nice, long contact list and accolades to my name.

I tug my cuff straight. "What do you need, sirs?" I'll repeat the question until I'm blue in the face. They'll get tired of wasting time eventually.

And sure enough: "One of the Briggs girls—she's a fresh little thing, just turned twenty two. She's starting some kind of cake business, and she needs an office as a base."

"An office," I say flatly. "For cakes."

"To sell them, not bake them. Apparently she's pitching to the grab-and-go crowd. Hungry workers chained to their desks."

"Oh, you're using chains now?" I shift in my seat, gusting out a sigh. "What does this have to do with me?"

For two busy men, they're dragging their feet on this explanation. Not a good omen.

"Her family is… protective of this one. They want someone looking after her at all times."

"They want a babysitter," I translate, my mouth suddenly bitter. Eight years of working here, for this? To become a glorified nanny to a spoiled rich girl?

"It's not for long," Vance breaks in, finding his tongue again at last. "Two weeks at most. This is a trial period—she'll use our firm as a base to test her products and prepare her business. Then she'll launch across the city and get out of our hair."

As one, Irving and I glance at the other man's bald head.

He scowls back at us, but for once, I don't care about soothing his ego.

I am a *lawyer.* A damn good one, too—the best in this building by far. I earned that partnership, and yet they're dangling it like a carrot, making me jump through this ridiculous hoop. Dios mío.

Enough messing around. "I want to make partner within three months."

"Done," Irving says quickly.

"Put that in writing and send me the full contract. The expected pay rise and bonus—everything. And I'll keep an eye on her, but that's it. I won't answer for whether her business flops or not, and I won't keep her *entertained.* I'm not taking her to the damn zoo."

Vance raises his palms. "It's barely anything, Julian. Escort her to and from the office each day. Keep an eye on her while she's here, and if she needs help or resources, lend her your assistant. Keep the Briggs girl happy."

Oliver is *my* assistant, damn it. He's an employee, not a stapler.

"Fine," I grit out. "Send the details over and have Oliver put her in my calendar."

"No need," Irving says. "You start tomorrow." I clench my jaw so hard my teeth ache.

Surely even *actual* babysitters get more warning than that.

Two

Lola

❧

When the intercom buzzes, I'm shoving one arm into a brightly patterned shirt and clutching a poppy seed bagel in the other. My pink hair is damp from the shower, and I changed my outfit four times already this morning before settling on high-waisted black leggings and a baggy shirt knotted at the waist. Is that too casual for an office? Should I add a necktie?

They're lawyers, Lola. Not the fashion police.

Too late now, anyway. My stomach's still twisted up like a pretzel, and I'm breathless when I abandon my bagel and stumble to the intercom. "Hello?"

"Lola Briggs?" The tinny voice is deep. Crackling with static.

"That's me."

A heavy sigh gusts through the speakers. "Alright, then. Let's go."

That's it. No 'good morning'. No 'your ride is here'. Just: let's go. And let me tell you, *no one* talks to the Briggs family like that. My all-powerful uncle would chew them into pieces and spit them out if they did, and woe betide anyone who insults his precious Lola. I'm *delicate*, see?

Ugh. It's the worst.

But hearing someone address me like a normal girl, like a regular pain in the ass–it's a weird little thrill. I kinda like this intercom grump.

"I'll be right down."

My outfit may be a lost cause, but I *am* prepared. I stayed up past midnight last night, checking and rechecking my supplies, then stacking them carefully by the door. I've spent the last few days making lists and schedules and plans. I. Am. Ready.

My first day! So exciting.

Since spending the last decade shut away in sterile rooms and private hospitals, I never did that first-day-of-college thing. I didn't go to parties or dates or cookouts, and I was never a regular teenager. I barely saw further than my yellow bedroom walls. And I'm twenty-two now, but I'm still greener than grass. I only moved out on my own two weeks ago, striking out into the big, wide world.

So maybe the nerves fizzing in my belly are totally normal; maybe it's common for my hands to shake and for me to barely fumble my apartment door open. Maybe a normal girl would clatter down the staircase like a moving disaster zone too, dropping a trail of colored markers and tubs of glitter behind her.

A man stands in the center of my building's lobby, watching me come downstairs, his face carefully blank.

My sandal slips on the final step. I stumble forward, dropping a sheet of poster board with a smack. The man sighs.

"Miss Briggs." It's not a question. It's the sound of a man resigned to his fate, and gosh, if someone handed me a pen and notepad and told me to draw a sexy lawyer, I'd definitely draw this guy. He's well muscled under his tailored clothes; he's tall and broad-shouldered. He looks expensive, like the human embodiment of fine brandy, with dark hair and smooth, light brown skin.

His scowl is harsh and his beard is sleek. Should I tell him I want to pet it?

Probably not.

A second man scurries across the lobby, and shoot, I didn't even see him standing back there. How could I when the scowling man takes up so much presence, like a black hole sucking all my attention? But this second guy darts me a smile, and he's way less intimidating. His suit is baggier, his chestnut curls flopping over his forehead, and freckles dust his pale cheeks.

"This is my assistant, Oliver. He'll help you in the office."

"Hi, Oliver. Thank you so much," I add, because the cutie's picking up my trail of debris from the stairs. I beam at him, and he blushes, fumbling my poster board.

Another deep sigh from the grump.

"Please be ready in the lobby at 7:30 sharp every morning."

I hitch several tote bags higher on my shoulder, the straps cutting into my collarbone. "Sure, okay. I'll be on time, I promise." He turns on his heel to leave, and I hurry after him. The street outside is cool, sunshine bathing the sidewalk, and pale white blossoms cling to a nearby tree.

"Um, sir?" He doesn't turn back, though I *know* he hears me. My sandals slap against the sidewalk as I chase him. "Sir? What should I call you?"

A small shrug. The grump leads us to a sleek black car, pulling the rear door wide, and gestures inside at plush leather seats.

"Courtesy of your uncle," he tells me. Then to really hammer home what he thinks of me: "Most people would walk the nine blocks."

I huff and squeeze past him, tumbling onto the backseat in a landslide of boxes and tote bags. I may not be sick anymore, but I haven't regained my strength either. Nine blocks? I might as well run a marathon. I'd turn up then need a three hour nap, but there's no way I'm telling the grump that.

"You didn't answer my question," I prod instead. "What should I call you?" Because somehow, I don't think 'sexy lawyer' will go down well.

It's Oliver who squeezes into the backseat beside me, juggling my dropped poster board and glitter tubs. The other man shuts the door on us with a thump, then slides into the front beside the driver.

He turns to face us. Draws his dark gaze over me from head to toe, lingering on my pink hair and knotted shirt with flamingos printed on it. My muddle of craft supplies and tote bags. The car pulls into the street, the cool air con tickling my warm cheeks.

"What do you usually call your nannies, Miss Briggs?"

Oh. Oh, he's *such* a jerk. Oliver winces beside me, but I ball my hands in my lap and hit the grump with my sweetest, don't-give-a-damn smile. I haven't had a nanny for years, but sure, I had them before I got sick. They were awesome, too. They're *still* awesome, and they all keep in touch. They all come to Briggs family barbecues. "Their names, of course. So what's your name, please?"

Skyscrapers slide past the car windows.

"Mr Rodriguez," he finally says.

I turn to Oliver. "You don't get a 'mister'?" Out of the corner of my eye, his boss bristles. I guess I shouldn't ignore him in favor of his assistant. Too bad, so sad.

"Oliver is fine." His assistant's blue eyes dart between us, back and forth, back and forth. He looks fascinated–like he's watching a tennis match.

I nudge Oliver with my elbow. "So is Lola. We'll be spending a lot of time together, right?"

There's a muffled snarl from the front seat. Somehow, I don't think Mr Rodriguez is too excited to be on Lola duty, but hey—I'm not thrilled with him either. I glare at the back of his perfect head as we drift through lanes of traffic, at the dark hair curling against his neck. He's so *strong* looking. Like he's been sculpted from marble.

Well, the man's gorgeous, but he's an asshole. A grade A jerk.

With any luck, I'll spend the next two weeks with Oliver and barely see this guy.

* * *

"Oh, good." Four hours later, a rich drawl curls through the office. I stiffen where I'm sitting cross-legged against the wall opposite Oliver's desk, pieces of poster board splayed out around me like a glittery fall out zone. The door to Mr Rodriguez's office has opened, and he's leaning in the doorway. His jacket is gone, and his shirtsleeves are rolled to the elbow. His forearms are corded with muscle where they cross over his chest. "It's arts and crafts hour. My favorite part of daycare."

Why? Why did I do this to myself? Why did I bring a bunch of crap into this office to *draw?* This idea made so much more

13

sense in my head, damn it. Sure, I came up with a bunch of logo designs on my own, but I wanted to play-test them. See how people responded to each one, then tweak in real time.

The end result? Day one, and I look like a crazy person. And I've spilled glitter *everywhere.*

"I'm working on logos," I tell Mr Rodriguez from behind the pink curtain of my hair. If I don't look at him, maybe he can't hurt me. Like a bogeyman. "To see which one customers like better."

He hums. "And busy lawyers are the perfect judges of design."

"They're my target audience," I say, though it sounds weak to my own ears. God, can I even do this? Starting a business is a really big step. It took me over an hour last night to order groceries. I kept getting overwhelmed and closing the website tab.

"You could have brought completed designs."

Yes. Yes, I could have. But I didn't do that, because I'm an idiot.

I blow out a shaky breath, and my poster boards blur in front of my watery eyes. Steps drum across the carpet, then buffed black leather shoes stop beside my crossed legs.

"Sprinkletown." Mr Rodriguez says it the same way he might say 'garbage patch'. This close, I catch the faint scent of his cologne–he smells warm and expensive and masculine.

Well, I guess two out of three isn't bad.

"You don't like the name?" I croak.

He hums, noncommittal.

"I like it," Oliver volunteers.

Thank god for sweet assistants. I shoot Oliver a grateful smile, and he jolts with concern at my damp eyes and blotchy cheeks. He opens his mouth to say something, but I shake my head quickly.

Please, no. Please don't give your boss anymore ammunition.

"Sprinkletown cupcakes," Mr Rodriguez drawls.

"Cake pops," I correct. "They're like lollipops, but, um, made of cake. They're more portable and less messy. Better for office workers."

A black shoe scuffs at the glitter now ingrained in the carpet. "Yes. In offices, we do hate mess."

"Sorry." Curled up on the floor, I feel about two inches tall. Like I'm shrinking down to live in the carpet like a flea. A glittery, fabulous flea. "I'll clean it up before I leave."

There's a grunt, and then he strides away, thank god. Off to bother Oliver about meetings and memos and other lawyer stuff. They mention a court date and my ears perk up—gosh, I watched so many legal dramas on the hospital wards—but I know better than to ask. Halfway into my first day, and my survival instincts have finally kicked in.

I sniffle quietly, tugging my favorite logo closer. This one, I think. This is the one I'll take to the break rooms for feedback.

* * *

Uncle Ray calls when we're in the car on the way home. Mr Rodriguez is in the front seat again, paging through a stack of papers on his lap, while Oliver types like crazy on his phone. They're definitely heading back to the office after this, and jeez, how late do they work? It's 5pm and I'm so tired, I'm a zombie. If I stayed out another minute, I'd start walking into walls.

"Hey, Uncle Ray." In the front seat, Mr Rodriguez stiffens. He stops shuffling his papers, blatantly eavesdropping, and usually I might take this chance to mess with him, but tonight, I'm too tired. "What's up?"

"Hey, Lola-Rose." He calls me that, even though it's not my name. Says it's because I'm pretty as a flower. All at once, homesickness slams into my chest so hard I can barely breathe.

There's no one waiting for me at home, not like when I lived on the Briggs family estate. No sweet uncles or aunts or cousins; just my dark, empty apartment, the silence so thick I can hear my own heartbeat.

"How was your first day? Were the lawyers nice to you?"

I stare at the back of Mr Rodriguez's head. He's so freaking obvious, listening in like that, but I don't want to argue with him. I don't want anything except maybe to lie my head in Aunt Hattie's lap and feel her stroke my hair while I fall asleep.

"It was good, thanks." My voice is small, so I clear my throat. Try to sound convincing. "I picked out a logo. And we settled on Sprinkletown."

"That's great, honey!" I slam my eyes shut, swallowing past the lump in my throat. What is wrong with me? Must be hormones or something. "And they were nice to you?" he asks again.

"They were nice," I whisper. Then cough, and speak louder. "Super nice. I–I worked with this guy Oliver today. He's the best. He's sitting right here, riding home with me."

I don't mention Mr Rodriguez, but I don't call him a jerk either. I'm not out to cause anyone trouble, and next to me, Oliver nudges me with a goofy smile.

"Good," Uncle Ray says, and he sounds relieved. "And you're not too tired? You don't feel dizzy? Don't forget, you can take as many days off as you need."

"I will," I say, even though I don't plan on slacking off. Everyone else may think this business is a hobby, a phase I'm going through, but I *really* want it to work. Can't make that happen by babying myself, can I? "Thanks for checking in, Uncle Ray."

"Any time, Lola-Rose."

I stare out of the window the rest of the way home.

Tomorrow will be better—that's what I always say. It's the mantra that got me through those hospital checks and rounds of treatment; it reminds me to think of bright, happy things.

Tomorrow will be better, and Sprinkletown cake pops will be awesome.

Mr Rodriguez will see.

Three

Julian

ꕥ

Day two of Lola-sitting, and I offer to fetch her alone. It's hardly a two man job, and this way my assistant can get a start on his day. On *our* day. But Oliver guffaws loudly at the offer and drops his briefcase on the desk, then turns on his heel and leads me to the elevator.

"That's not a good idea, Mr Rodriguez."

I follow, mouth pressed in a flat line. Why did I make such a point of telling Oliver he could challenge me whenever he liked? That I value his input? Clearly that was a mistake.

"Why not? It's nine blocks and a ditsy girl with pink hair. I think I can handle her."

Oliver jabs the elevator button and throws me a look over his shoulder. "That's what I'm afraid of. You already made her cry once, and I'm not going to watch you ruin your career just because you're pissy about Lola being here. I don't want to work for these other lawyers, Mr Rodriguez. They're boring."

18

Julian

"I did not make her cry." I step inside the elevator beside Oliver, glaring at the shorter man. I did *not* do that. I think I would have fucking noticed.

Noticed, and gone easier on her. I'm an asshole but not a monster.

"She cleaned the carpet," Oliver says. "The glitter's almost gone."

I huff. "She did not cry."

"I saw her." He frowns at the panel of floor buttons, watching them light up one by one as we descend. "When you were bitching at her about arts and crafts."

Oh, come on. That was ridiculous. Who brings glitter tubs and poster board to a professional office? Who wears flamingo printed shirts and dyes their hair pink? This is a law firm, not a festival ground.

"I do not *bitch*."

The look Oliver levels at me speaks a thousand words. I grunt, tugging my jacket sleeves straight.

Maybe I was harsh. I certainly didn't get this far in life by rolling over and showing my belly—I've fought tooth and nail for every victory. And there are days when this place feels more like a battleground than a law firm.

Maybe I should lower my weapons. At least with Miss Briggs.

After all, I don't come after Oliver like a snarling tiger, and he's the best assistant I've ever had. There's something to be said for that trust, the camaraderie that comes from *not* trying to one up each other and stab each other in the back all the time.

What is this? Is Oliver using this as a teachable moment?

I watch him out of the corner of my eye. My assistant is wearing a salmon pink shirt today, and it matches the constant flush on his cheeks. "Are you managing me again?"

"Yes," he says simply, smiling brightly as we step into the Irving & Vance lobby. Our shoes echo against the marble tiles, and through the glass doors, the car service idles by the sidewalk. "You can thank me later, Mr Rodriguez."

I should ship this kid back to HR.

* * *

Nine blocks is a ridiculous distance to order a car service, especially since the morning traffic is almost as slow as walking. Who is she, royalty? When we step out onto the sidewalk at her building, the vicious comments are already lined up on my tongue. I swallow them back, the cool morning breeze ruffling my hair. The street smells like asphalt and ozone.

Maybe Oliver's right. Maybe I was too hard on Lola. I fiddle with my collar, annoyed, as we step into the lobby.

I fully expect her to run late. For us to buzz the intercom again, and then to watch her clatter down the stairs with another armful of ridiculous supplies. Finger paints, maybe, or a tie-dying kit.

Instead, Lola's waiting in the lobby with a single cardboard box in her arms. She's dressed more demurely today, in a gray button down shirt tucked into black pants, and she looks tired. Dark shadows cling to her eyes, and her lips are pale.

Her hair's still pink, thank god. But drawn back in a low bun.

"Miss Briggs." There's an uncomfortable tug in my chest as I take her in. "You're on time. Good."

She nods, but she won't meet my eye–though she smiles at Oliver as she trails past. He offers to take the box from her arms and she refuses politely, leading us out onto the sidewalk.

Where the hell is Lola Briggs, and who is this tired, sad, monochromatic girl? Where did all that color and life go? She was only with us for one day!

Fuck. I really am a monster.

Oliver beats me to the car, so he gets to open the door for her. She smiles again and thanks him, settling herself gingerly on the back seat. Is she in pain? What is happening here?

I slide into the back seat before Oliver has a chance. There's a huff of laughter, and then the door closes behind me with a thump.

Lola glances over, and jerks when she finds me instead of Oliver. I don't examine the bitter possessiveness that snakes through me at that. Is my assistant really so much better? He's friendly, yes, but like a golden retriever. Bouncy and often irritating.

"Oh. Um. Good morning, Mr Rodriguez."

"Good morning, Miss Briggs." I scan her from up close, then peer into her cardboard box. Lola flips the lid shut, her lips pursed.

Oliver climbs in beside the driver, and we pull away, then coast through the morning traffic, the car silent and sleek. The driver's listening to the radio, the news bulletin almost impossibly quiet, and Oliver chats with him about some college football game.

I stare at the shadows under Lola's eyes. "Did you sleep well?"

She peeks at me, then away. Frowns out of the window, her pulse tapping in her throat. "I slept fine, thank you."

Liar. "You look tired."

Lola scoffs. I wait, but apparently that's all she's giving me. A scoff. What does that *mean*?

"No arts and crafts today?"

21

Her mouth twists, but she says nothing.

"You did a good job with the carpet," I offer.

Lola nods, still staring out of the window instead of at me. "Maybe I'll open a cleaning business instead of Sprinkletown."

"That's a pity. It's a good name."

Finally, she looks at me. Steals a glance to check whether I'm mocking her or if I mean it. And I mean it, okay? I thought about it a lot last night. The name grew on me... and so did Lola.

Fuck, did I really make her cry? I haven't felt this shitty since I yelled at Oliver for spilling coffee on my case notes.

Oliver forgave me, though, especially after I apologized loudly to him in the break room, then offered him a long weekend to go visit his parents. So maybe Lola's not a lost cause either.

"You don't need to worry, Mr Rodriguez." Hope bubbles up inside me just in time to be popped. "I won't get you fired, and we can spend the next two weeks staying as far away from each other as possible. Maybe tomorrow, Oliver could fetch me alone."

She thinks I'm groveling for my job? Hell no. Julian Rodriguez does not crawl for anything, and he certainly doesn't beg little girls not to run to their big, scary uncle. Who the fuck does she think she's dealing with? How does my career hang on this stupid situation? Why does she want to be alone with Oliver so badly?

Resentment simmers in me, toxic and hot.

"That's good," I say, and I can't stop the vicious words as they punch out of me. Somewhere in the back of my head, the conscience that sounds suspiciously like Oliver screams at me to stop talking. "I would hate for you to cause more trouble than you're worth, Miss Briggs. God forbid you waste anyone's time. But hey, you have a powerful uncle, right? So I suppose that makes *you* worthwhile. Oliver and I would be lucky to kiss your feet."

No sandals today, I note. No sparkly blue toe nails. Plain black ballet flats.

All at once, I deflate. Regret is sour in my mouth.

I've done it again. Taken my frustrations with Irving & Vance out on this girl—who already looks like she's weathered a few blows today, and it's not even 8am. Her shoulders curled over as I talked, and now she looks even smaller, lost in the wasteland of plush black leather car seats.

My chest throbs.

"Listen, Lola—"

Her fingers tighten on the box until the cardboard creaks. Her voice is a whisper. "Please don't."

Ah, shit. I feel like something sticky on her shoe. Her sensible, tragic little shoe.

Outside the car, the buildings sliding past are familiar. We're nearing the office, and *no*, I can't let her scurry away from me like this, all hurt and rumpled and small.

"I'm sorry," I say quickly, wincing as I sense Oliver stop chatting to listen in. "That was uncalled for, Miss Briggs. I am a little… frustrated by our current situation, but it's nothing you've done. Forgive me. Oliver can tell you—I am not a morning person."

"He's not," Oliver choruses helpfully from the front seat. "One time I brought him a breakfast muffin and he tossed it in the garbage."

Lola's eyebrows flick up.

"It smelled like death," I tell her. I won't be unfairly maligned. "Truly awful. And he smeared ketchup on my office door handle."

Oliver snorts, and Lola's lips twitch, and my heart thumps harder in response. It feels like victory. Like winning a case in court. I grin at her and she smiles back, shy and unsure.

I'll take it. God, I'll take it. Not because I'm scared of her damn uncle, but because I hate seeing this girl hurt. And I hate even worse knowing that I'm the asshole responsible.

"All meat smells like death if you think about it," my assistant muses. When the car slows outside the office, I leap out and beat Oliver to Lola's door, holding it open for her and avoiding his eye.

His knowing gaze still makes the back of my neck itch all the way up to the office.

It's a relief to shut myself away and leave the two of them out there together.

Four

Lola

Oliver connects my laptop to the internet and gets me settled on the end of his desk. It's a large table, all glass and chrome, and I wince as my rolling chair squeaks with every movement. My cardboard box is tucked away by my feet.

"Are you sure I'm not bothering you here?"

Oliver shakes his head, scrolling through Mr Rodriguez's calendar. Even with my partial view of the screen, I can see his boss is a very busy man.

A busy, bad-tempered... sometimes sweet man. A powerful man who knows how to apologize. Seriously! I thought those were a myth.

"Don't worry about it, Lola. It's nice to have some company here besides his Highness."

I hide my smile behind my hand, clicking away at my own screen. Pulling up the detailed customer survey I compiled last

25

week.

Okay.

Okay.

I check my email. Send off a photo of my chosen logo mock-up to the graphic designer I picked out. Check the news. Look up nearby noodle bars for lunch.

But finally, I can't escape reality anymore. The whole reason I'm *here* instead of working at home on my sofa is so I can do market research. So I can trial designs and flavors and ideas, and eventually, force feed these lawyers free samples.

Oliver chuckles when I collapse on the desk, face squished against my folded arms. How can I go out there and talk to all those serious, professional people? What if they all hate me like Mr Rodriguez? "Feeling shy of the scary lawyers?"

I nod, bun wobbling. "Uh-huh. I need to ask them to fill out a survey."

"Don't worry. They won't bite."

I puff out a breath. A strand of my hair keeps sticking to the corner of my mouth. "Because of my uncle," I say flatly, the words echoing weirdly against the glass table. Isn't that what Mr Rodriguez implied this morning? That my presence here is a pain, and not a freely given favor like Uncle Ray told me? So humiliating.

"Well," Oliver says. "Yeah." My heart sinks to somewhere near my toes, but Oliver shoves his chair back. "Come on, I'll go with you. Mr Rodriguez can answer his own calls for an hour or two."

The last thing I need is more reasons for that man to hate me... but the temptation of company is too much to resist.

"We'll go to the break rooms." Oliver tugs me to my feet. "We won't be interrupting anyone there. And shit, people love talking about food, Lola. Plus these are some of the most opinionated assholes you'll ever find." I trail him to the printer against the wall, jabbing at buttons until warm white copies of my survey start spitting out into the tray.

Oliver sucks in a deep breath, waving a hand by his face like a sommelier. "God, yeah. I love the smell of toner in the morning."

I bark out a loud laugh, glancing nervously at Mr Rodriguez's closed door. Behind the polished wood, his deep voice rumbles as he talks on the phone.

"He said he likes the name Sprinkletown."

Oliver's grin is wider than the Cheshire cat's. "Oh, yeah. I bet he does."

* * *

Two hours and eighty three completed surveys later, Oliver and I step out of the elevator, laughing. It's been so *nice* hearing people say they like my idea. That it's the kind of sweet treat they might actually buy. Not everyone said that, obviously, but enough did that I feel like less of an idiot.

And maybe this could work. Maybe it's not a crazy whim like everyone thinks. Because this is only one office building, but there are so many more out there. In this block, this postcode, this *city*. If I could sell my cake pops in even a few of those places, if I could get the Sprinkletown name out there, maybe…

Maybe I could build something all by myself. Could actually make something of my sheltered life.

Mr Rodriguez is waiting in his open doorway. He's scowling at Oliver's empty desk, but he transfers that stink-eye to us when he hears us coming.

God, he looks angry. And tall. And hot. His dark eyes sear into me, and goosebumps prickle over my skin.

"Where have you two been?" he grits out.

I wave my clipboard at him, completed surveys fluttering. "I asked Oliver to help me with these. I'm sorry I took him away from his work." No way am I letting Oliver take the fall for this one—he made going into all those break rooms so much easier. It's like he has a superpower for handling grumpy lawyers.

Mr Rodriguez snaps his fingers, then gestures for my clipboard. I carry it over to him, choking back a laugh. "Oh my god. Are you one of those people who click their fingers at servers?"

He takes my clipboard. Flips through the papers with a frown. "Of course not. What is this?"

"A survey. About cake pops."

Brown eyes flick to me, then back down. After a second, I remember to breathe again. "Naturally." Then the world tilts on its axis, because Mr Rodriguez draws a pen from his pocket and starts ticking boxes on a fresh sheet.

"Um."

He ignores me, scrawling a detailed answer to one of my questions.

"Don't worry," Oliver calls. "I'll help you read his shitty handwriting."

The frown deepens, but Mr Rodriguez keeps writing. Determined not to stare at his cheekbones like a weirdo, I read the bronze plaque on his office door.

Julian Rodriguez.

"I like the name Julian." Another fleeting glance leaves me tingling.

"And I like Sprinkletown." Lord, his voice is deep. Rich and smooth, like melted chocolate. "So I suppose we're even."

This is so different compared to yesterday. Compared to frosty, pointed silences and his black leather shoe scraping my glitter over the carpet. I can't help beaming at him, practically bouncing on my toes, and when Mr Rodriguez hands back my clipboard, he looks a little alarmed.

"Get some work done, Oliver," he clips over my shoulder, then to me: "If you need anything else, knock on my door, Miss Briggs." He shoots a final sour look at his chuckling assistant, then shuts the door gently in my face.

* * *

"Be honest with me. How late do you two work?"

It's just past 5pm, and we're stepping out into the street. It's a warm evening, the sky's still light, and music floats out from a nearby bar. The sidewalk is thick with pedestrians running past in two streams, and I hurry after Mr Rodriguez as he cuts a path to the car, my box balanced under one of his toned arms.

"I'll get out of here in an hour or so," Oliver calls from a few steps back. "*That* guy probably sleeps at his desk."

Mr Rodriguez pulls the car door open for me and doesn't deign to snipe back at his assistant. But when Oliver tries to slide in beside me, a big hand clamps on his shoulder and steers him to the front of the car.

I watch Mr Rodriguez settle in the car beside me, butterflies dancing in my belly. He glances over, and seems relieved when I offer him a smile.

"I don't sleep at my desk," he says after a long moment, when the car pulls away. His legs are so long, folded in the back like this. He must have been more comfortable when he sat in the front. "But Oliver can't imagine my existence when he's not

29

there."

I bite the inside of my cheek. These two are such an odd pair.

"It must be lonely for him," his assistant sighs, shaking his head. His chestnut curls flutter in the air con. "So cold and gray."

Mr Rodriguez's eyes crinkle when he sees my lips twitch. And I'm filing all this away, rewriting the story of this man in my head to someone who lets his assistant sass him freely. Who's grumpy and strict and demanding, yes, but who has a sense of humor too.

He's downright indulgent with Oliver, though his assistant can only be five or so years younger. What must that be like—being one of Julian Rodriguez's soft spots?

A wave of longing crashes over me, and an ache throbs in my chest.

Just imagine it. God.

Five

Julian

After a week of Lola-sitting, I'm… acclimatized. It's automatic, when I arrive in the office on Monday, to drop my briefcase on my desk then march Oliver down to the car service, sweeping out into the traffic and crossing the nine blocks to her door. I haven't suggested again that he leave me to fetch her alone, and he hasn't offered.

Would Lola like that? Would it make her uncomfortable? Is Oliver protecting her from me? She hasn't been so tense around me lately, but god knows we got off on the wrong foot.

Fuck, I hate that idea. That Lola might find me frightening.

It's strange, because in my work, having a fearsome reputation can only be a good thing. I *want* my competitors—and some of my colleagues, too—to get sweaty palms at the thought of facing me. I've taken great care over the years to establish myself as merciless. A cold-hearted bastard with a killer instinct.

But I sure as hell don't want Lola to think of me like that. The thought makes my throat tight.

"Free samples this week." Oliver is practically giddy with glee, his knee jiggling as we share the back seat. "I asked Lola for double chocolate."

I resist the urge to cuff the back of his head. "You shouldn't give her extra work." She looked tired enough on Friday night after four full days at the office. After more market research and web design and all the exhausting nuts and bolts of starting a business. She was pale and gaunt, collapsing into the car service with a sigh of relief, her slender body drowning in another soulless button down shirt and sensible dark pants.

I did that. I stomped the color out of her on her first day.

What I wouldn't give to see that flamingo-print blouse again. We only have one more week to make that dream come true.

"It's not extra work," Oliver huffs. "I'm an office worker who loves sugar and snack foods that come on sticks. I'm her target demographic, and *I* love double chocolate. We don't all subsist on push ups and repression," he adds quietly, and maybe I really will smack him.

Oliver slides into the front seat while I meet Lola in the lobby. Her building is large and grand, my footsteps echoing off polished tiles, and she holds her palms up as soon as she sees me.

"Please don't be mad."

See what I mean? There's a lot I need to fix between Lola and I. She's squirming with anxiety as I come closer, my hands tucked in my pockets as I survey the giant suitcase at her side. Though she's dressed in gray and black again, her luggage is pure Lola. It's candy pink, with turquoise zips and handles.

Seeing that case is like finding water in the desert.

"Nice case." I grab the handle and start rolling it toward the street. Lola scurries after me, her pink head bobbing in the corner of my eye.

"I'm sorry it's so huge, Mr Rodriguez."

"Julian," I tell her.

"It's just, I wanted to bring enough samples to go around the whole building. To be efficient, you know? Then I'll be out of your way sooner."

My grip tightens on the suitcase handle. I keep my gaze fixed on the car waiting for us in the street. "There's no need to rush."

Lord, please don't let her rush. I want the full two weeks with Lola, and not a day less. She could move her whole apartment into my office and I'd still feel the same.

I roll her suitcase out of the lobby and across the sidewalk, leaning over to pop the trunk of the car. It takes me a minute to wedge the case inside–it really is a beast–and when I slam the trunk shut, Lola is still there. Watching me with those big, blue eyes.

I grin, rounding the car. "You couldn't open your own door?"

A few days ago, there would have been an edge to those words, and Lola would have flinched, a blush climbing her throat.

This morning, she laughs, waiting for me to hold the door open before sliding inside. Her body passes close to mine, separated only by a hunk of metal, and I catch a whiff of her vanilla scent.

"I like when you do it," Lola murmurs before ducking inside the car.

I stand on the sidewalk for a long moment, heart hammering. Did she really say that?

Jesus.

Once we're all folded inside the car, I clear my throat, thumb tapping against my knee. We pull into traffic, slow and easy. She likes when I do it? When I hold the car door? What else would she like me to do for her? Images batter my brain—a slideshow of carrying things for Lola and winding a scarf around her neck and fuck, lifting her up to see a high shelf—when Oliver pipes up from the front seat.

"Did you bring double chocolate ones?"

Ugh.

I slide lower in my seat and stare out of the window, face hot.

* * *

Lola props the suitcase against the wall opposite Oliver's desk. I should go inside my own office and tackle the landslide of work waiting for me there, but instead I linger, peering over Lola's shoulder. She's kneeling, the lid of the suitcase flipped open, inspecting the dozens of clear plastic containers filled with cake pops for signs of damage.

"You baked a lot this weekend."

"Uh-huh." Lola lifts a box of samples from the back row. They're pink with sprinkles.

"Make sure you take some breaks. You look a little tired." God, this is like Oliver's first week as my assistant. He accused me of trying to baby him, and I scoffed and offered him a game of catch. But Lola's not offended, thank god, because she sits back on her heels and offers me a sunny smile.

"Don't worry, Mr Rodriguez."

"Julian."

A huffed laugh. "Don't worry, Julian. I'm just trying to cram as much into my time here as possible. I'll take a few days off before I launch for real."

I hope so. And I hope I'm around for that somehow. Will she

sell her treats in this building? Or will she be sick of us by then?

If she takes her business elsewhere, will she stay in touch? Two weeks never felt so damn short.

"It's not long, is it?" Lola says quietly, and I guess we were thinking similar things. "I'm trying to cram a whole self-taught Business 101 course into a couple of weeks, but god knows if I'm on the right track. Most days I feel like a kindergartner pasting stuff to her head."

I hate the defeated slump to her shoulders. "You'll figure it out. You're a smart girl."

Lola smiles up at me again then, and too late, I realize how we're positioned–with me looming over her, and Lola on her knees at my feet. Blood pounds in my temples, and…elsewhere in my body, and I crouch quickly, bringing myself down to her level.

Behind us, Oliver taps away at his keyboard, gusting out one of the heavy sighs he saves for Mondays.

Lola makes a little squeak when I pluck her hand, wrapping it in both of mine. She seems flustered but pleased, and I hold her hand close to my chest. Oliver stops typing, but I don't care.

It's the first time we've touched. The first time I've felt her slender fingers, her pulse thrumming beneath the thin skin of her wrist.

"You're very warm," Lola murmurs.

Yes, that happens around her.

"You can do this, Lola." I squeeze her hand gently, and watch her shy smile bloom in response. "You can overcome any setback, and you *will* make Sprinkletown a success. I have faith in you," I add quietly, squeezing her hand one more time before I let it go.

When I push to my feet, Oliver's gaze makes my neck itch. I

can't look at him, or Lola, or anything except my office door.

"Don't disturb me this morning," I clip out, striding to the safety of my office.

I close the door on their replies.

* * *

It's 4pm, and I've had no samples. I want a cake pop, damn it, but I made such a stupid fuss about being left in my fortress of solitude that of course Lola didn't bring me one. Should I go poking around the break rooms? Or maybe Oliver has some on his desk. I pace up and down beside the glass wall of my office, the late afternoon sunshine warm on my cheeks.

Before Lola came here, I was so obsessed with my work that sometimes I'd forget to eat. I was a machine, a deadly, relentless machine, and my competitors had to live with the knowledge that while they were eating or sleeping or tending to their pathetic bodily needs, I was coming for them.

I'm not anymore.

Or rather, I *am*—I'm still doing my damn work. I'm still one of the best. But I'm not obsessed like I was, not single-minded in my pursuit.

Not with the law, anyway.

"Double chocolate," I mutter, tugging at my collar. I'm in a waistcoat and shirt, my sleeves rolled to the elbow, and the tie is the next to go. I can barely fucking breathe with Lola in this building, especially with this stupid scrap of silk choking me to death.

Oliver requested a flavor from her. I bet he got the first samples too. They're *close*, chatting all day out there, and lord knows she's spent far more time with him than with me. He's nearer her age, too.

...Does she like him? Does Lola have a crush on my assistant?

I snarl, tugging at my tie and working the knot tighter. I'm so busy growling and pacing and yanking at my clothes that I don't even hear the door nudge open behind me.

"Um." I whirl around and find Lola staring, wide-eyed. There's a tray balanced on her palms, with cake pops spread over white china plates. "Is this a bad time? Should I..." she trails off, blinking at the tie yanked part way around my throat.

Then she breathes out a laugh, and sets her tray down on top of a cabinet.

Lola approaches me like I'm a wild animal caught in a snare. I suppose she's not wrong.

"I always thought lawyers were so clever," my maddening girl says, plucking my tie out of my grip and working the knot loose. She's so fucking close, I can see each dark, curling eyelash; can see the delicate blue veins beneath her skin of her wrists.

When Lola shakes her head, biting back a smile, her pink ponytail rustles. Vanilla washes over me.

"This is no good." I slide her hair tie out before she can stop me, her strands silky against my knuckles. Pink waves fall to her shoulders, and Lola gazes up at me, breath held. Now we're even, freeing each other from these binds. "Pretty hair like yours should be loose. You wore it down on your first day."

Lola shrugs, but her cheeks are flushed as she goes back to fiddling with my tie. "I'm trying to look professional."

"Well, stop it." I pinch the collar of her gray shirt and give it a tug. "I miss the flamingos. All those bright colors. Please, Lola, I can't go on."

"So dramatic," she murmurs, and my necktie slithers through my collar. She pulls it out slowly, the motion tugging me gently

37

toward her. "Are you like this in court, Julian?"

"Of course." Her hips fit my palms so neatly. Lola doesn't push me away, not even when I step so close our chests brush. "When in doubt, strip. They teach that in the final year of law school."

Her laugh puffs warm against my throat. I squeeze her hips, biting back a groan.

"I brought you samples," Lola whispers.

"In a moment." God, I'd eat anything she brought me. Anything at all. But for now, I have my hands on her, and I've been waiting for this since the moment we met. She's *here*, pressed so close, gazing up at me with such trust, and the only thing I want to swallow whole is Lola Briggs.

But first: "What do you think of Oliver?"

She blinks, confused. "Oh, um. Your assistant? He's—he's nice—"

I swoop down and claim her mouth, chest rioting. She doesn't want him, which means there's still a chance that one day she'll want *me*. Julian Rodriguez, the declawed tiger. I kiss her like I'm stating my case, like I'm presenting exhibit A for why she should consider keeping me.

Lola sucks in a shocked breath, but then she grips my shoulders. Kisses me back. Her body bows against mine, every point of contact scorching through my clothes, and her mouth is hot, her lips soft, her breaths shallow.

I trail my palms up her waist, her ribs, her arms. When I trace my thumbs up her throat, her pulse pounds beneath her pale skin.

"Lola," I murmur against her mouth.

Her whimper is so sweet, I have to kiss it away.

Fuck. Kissing her... it's like nothing else in the world. It crackles up the length of my spine. I feel it in the roots of my hair.

We don't break apart until there are voices outside the open doorway. Oliver greets someone loudly—one of the bosses, by the sound of it, and Lola and I spring apart, smoothing our clothes and staring at the next room.

"Shit. I need—"

"It's fine," she says quickly, hurrying to the cabinet and rescuing her tray. "You can try them another day."

No!

Jesus Christ. So close to a cake pop. My stomach twists, miserably empty, but I scrub a hand over my jaw. Watching the flash of pink hair as she leaves, the jagged pieces inside me settle.

It's okay. It's okay. I'll try one soon.

Today, I tasted something much sweeter.

Six

Lola

You don't get much chance for romance on hospital wards. Kisses are the last thing on anyone's minds when you're surrounded by all those pale linoleum corridors and bright lights and beeping machines, so I passed my teenage years with zero experience. Untouched and unwanted—in that way, anyway.

When I was seventeen or so, I had this all-consuming crush on one of my doctors. He was Canadian, with this floppy blond hair, and he looked like he'd wandered out of a music video. But when I finally confessed my love to him during an appointment, he patted my hand, said 'thank you, Lola', then practically sprinted out into the hallway. He always brought a nurse with him to see me after that.

Talk about embarrassing. What was I thinking, telling a fully grown man that I wanted him?

I may be an adult now, but honestly, up until yesterday, I'd filed my fixation on Julian Rodriguez under the same category. The never-gonna-happen box. The you're-kidding-yourself-Lola file. The just-buy-a-vibrator-damn-it section.

I mean, he's a lawyer. A grumpy, scary, freaking *gorgeous* lawyer in his thirties, who has a fancy office and can grow a proper beard. And me? I dragged a suitcase around yesterday filled with hundreds of cake pops. I spilled glitter on his office carpet.

Sure, I got all flushed and tingly from pretty much the moment I met Julian, but I never dreamed that he might want *me.* Half the time, I still feel like that awkward girl on the ward. The one that people only spoke to in hushed tones.

But Julian's never been careful with me—not in that stifling way. And lord knows he didn't go easy on me to begin with.

He's softer with me now, but it doesn't feel like pity.

It's because he wants me. He really does.

It was all in that kiss.

* * *

"Good morning, sunshine." Oliver beams as he walks into my building's lobby, spreading his arms wide like we've been apart for weeks, not hours. The street is sunny behind him, and Oliver's dressed in a crisp white shirt. "The boss had to take a call, so we're riding solo this morning."

I nod and force a smile, dragging another suitcase of samples across the tiles. Oliver takes the handle neatly, leading me out onto the sidewalk. "Some of these have my name on them, Lola."

I hum in agreement, following him out into the cool breeze, but I can't think straight. Julian's not here? Did he really have a

41

call, or is he avoiding me?

Oh, god. He's like that Canadian doctor, sprinting away down the hospital hallway. I feel sick.

"You should give Mr Rodriguez a cake pop today." Oliver pops the trunk, heaving the suitcase inside with far less grace than Julian did. The car dips beneath the weight. "He was such a bitch when he didn't get one yesterday."

So is that it? He's mad that I didn't give him samples? Except no, I *did* bring him a tray, and he spent that time kissing me instead.

Cradling my jaw and sliding his tongue into my mouth; nipping my bottom lip and growling low in his chest. Pressing his hard body against me.

Oh, god. My head spins as I topple into the back seat. I'm not equipped for any of this. Oliver slides in beside me, closing the door with a thump, then starts chatting happily as we pull away from the sidewalk. After a minute he eyes me carefully, then clearly realizes that I'm barely listening, because he leans forward and mutters to the driver instead.

Julian's not here. He's *always* here.

He kissed me yesterday, and now he's stayed away. Is that a coincidence? Or does he regret it already?

* * *

Julian really is on the phone. He's been talking for *hours,* his deep voice rumbling through his closed office door all morning. Even from the next room, you can hear the impatient edge to his voice—and who can blame him? He must be thirsty. Must want to stretch his legs and find something to eat.

So he's grumpy. I shiver, though my skin is hot under my

clothes.

My nerves aside, I like when Julian is grumpy.

I took a risk today. After he pleaded with me to bring the color back, I stuffed the boring, drab clothes from last week to the back of my closet. This morning I'm back in my leggings and sandals and another baggy, bright shirt knotted at the waist. This one is light blue with a watermelon pattern.

"I'm gonna do it," I tell Oliver. "If he throws his pens at me, I'll toss a cake pop in his lap."

Oliver snorts. "You're a brave soul."

It's not *really* scary going in to see Julian. I fix him a plate with a powdered cake pop and make him a coffee with the fancy machine, then fumble his door open with my elbow.

Julian spins around in his desk chair with a scowl.

When he sees my bright shirt, his scowl melts and his gaze heats.

"Yes," Julian snaps down the phone. "We've been over this. It's not admissible in court." His eyes follow me as I nudge the door closed with my hip, then pad across his room.

Jeez, he looks good today. Like a man in a cologne advert, but gruffer. Real. Flesh and blood and a crisp, tailored shirt, watching me come closer like a cat watches a mouse. He grits something else down the phone, some annoyed legal jargon, and I set the coffee and plate on his desk.

"A snack," I whisper.

"At last. My fucking cake pop," he hisses back, and my cheeks ache, I'm grinning so hard. This is the part where I should leave—where I should go take my samples round the building and leave Julian in here to get some work done.

I don't turn to leave.

Julian's hand finds my hip. He kneads me, his thumb digging

into my tight muscles through my leggings.

"Well tell her the offer expires tonight. She can cover her losses, or she can go down with the rest of them."

With a tug, I'm drawn down onto Julian's lap.

I've stared at his thighs a *lot* over the last week. At all of his body, really. And I knew, somehow, that they'd be rock hard and sculpted. I shift against his leg, trying to get comfy, gripping the desk for balance.

Muffled words float down the phone.

"No shit," Julian barks. "Life's not fair. I'm a lawyer, not a fairy godmother. I hope you're not relying on my bleeding heart. At least make this interesting for me."

Ha. He's kind of a jerk when he's doing the lawyer thing. Scratch that—he's a jerk when he does lots of things, but not to me.

As if he can hear my thoughts, Julian wraps an arm around my waist, tugging me close until my back presses against his chest. He rests his chin on my shoulder with a quiet sigh. Like I'm a comfort.

The voice ranting down the phone sounds tinny. Super boring.

I play with the strip of Julian's wrist peeking from his cuff. It's so solid and broad. Dark hairs dust his golden brown skin, and tendons shift as his thumb moves, stroking my belly. When I shift, it slips under my shirt and finds bare skin.

God. I could purr right now. I squeeze my legs together, all tingly and restless. Julian grunts, then sets the phone down on the desk and presses a button to put it on speaker.

"The date is non-negotiable." Julian watches me carefully as he nudges me to my feet. I step between his thighs, turning so my ass rests against the edge of the desk. He lounges in his chair, dragging his gaze from my bare painted toes all the way up to my loose pink waves.

"Be reasonable, Mr Rodriguez. That is not enough time to prepare." The voice behind me makes me jump. I forgot I can hear it all now—and they can hear me. I press my lips together, staring into fierce brown eyes.

"But it is enough." Julian smooths his palms up my outer thighs, my hips, my waist. He's mapping me, heavy eyebrows pinched in a scowl, and it's so freaking *possessive*—like he owns me. "Our team can manage it. Why can't yours?"

I clench my thighs again, choking back a whimper.

Julian smirks.

A sigh rattles down the phone. "We're making no headway here."

Julian tugs on the knotted ends of my shirt. "I disagree." The sides come loose, held together only by two buttons. Julian flicks them open, holding my gaze.

I want to giggle. Want to moan, want to gasp, want to say *something*, but I can't. All I can do is grip the desk tight and watch as Julian opens my shirt, his hot gaze licking over my bare skin like a tongue.

My belly button. My stomach rising and falling with each breath. The lilac lace of my bralette—Julian soaks it all up like it's the best thing he's ever seen. When he flattens a palm on my body, fingers spreading wide, it's like he's marking me. Locking me to his fingerprints.

He doesn't seem to care at all about the angry voice on the phone, or his assistant sitting just outside that door, or anything except leaning forward and pressing his bearded cheek to the bare skin of my chest.

"Vanilla," he murmurs.

"What?" says the voice.

"Nothing," Julian snaps. He grips the sides of my waist, holding me close. It's like he's listening to my heartbeat, but that can't be difficult. My heart's pounding so loud, even I can hear it. "Do you have anything useful to give me today, or is your whole plan simply to waste my time until you've run out the clock?"

There's an outraged huff, and then the line goes dead. My penned up giggles explode out of me, and Julian leans back and chuckles, one thumb rubbing the lace above my nipple. I suck in a breath, arching into his touch. "Honestly, these lawyers have such thin skins. They're exhausting, Lola."

I weave my fingers through his dark hair. "Tell me about it."

Our kiss is fierce. Hot and demanding, all teeth and tongues. Any doubts I had this morning are long gone—he wants me as badly as ever. Worse, even, and when I come up for air, the sight of his arousal pressing against his fly makes my breath stutter.

"Your coffee will go cold."

Julian cups my breast again, kneading harder. "I don't care."

I rock my hips against nothing, whimpering when he pinches my hard nipple. "Ungrateful jerk."

God. He's hot and big and muscled and bossy. He's *everywhere*, invading all of my senses. Julian growls and surges closer, desk chair creaking, trapping me between his thighs—and I'm so caught up in the moment that I don't notice the plate sliding until it's too late.

Thump. It bounces, thank god, but powdered sugar explodes across the carpet. Julian and I stare down at the mess, his grip still tight on my waist, and a muscle leaps in his jaw.

For a horrible moment, I think he might yell at me.

Lola

Then: "Shit." His forehead thumps against my collarbone. "Lola, Lola. Beautiful Lola. Destroyer of carpets. When will I get you alone?"

The planes of his back are toned and broad beneath his shirt. His warmth seeps through the fabric, and I rub soothing circles over his shoulder blades, my insides all jelly. "Um. Well, you know where I live."

Is that desperate? Do I sound needy? God, I don't know, but Julian seems pleased with my answer. He nods once, brisk, then lets me go. Pushes to his feet and stares down at the powdered sugar on his floor.

"I'll clean it," I say quickly, but he's already waving a hand.

"Don't worry. It was my fault."

"But I—"

"Go take your samples around," he says, tucking a lock of pink hair behind my ear. His mouth quirks up. "Time for Sprinkletown."

I smile, but there's a sharp ache in my gut. I *hate* leaving him, hate retying my shirt and stepping out of that office back into reality.

Oliver raises an eyebrow at me, but I march to my suitcase, avoiding his eye and fighting the urge to smooth down my hair.

I'm not gonna start any rumors about Julian. Lord knows I've caused enough trouble.

Seven

Julian

⁓◦⸎◦⁓

Once again, I am the only soul at Irving & Vance not to taste one of Lola's sweet little cake pops. I've tasted other things, of course—her lips, her sugared breath, her warm, bare skin—but still. It rankles.

I shouldn't go to her apartment. It's late, and she needs rest, but I've denied myself all pleasures for so long that our kiss has opened my flood gates. I'm weakened. Desperate for more. My system is overwhelmed.

I curse my own name, standing on the sidewalk and staring at her buzzer. It's old fashioned, made of bronze. Her place is very nice, as befits the Briggs family fortune.

Lola's first apartment is more expensive than any I could afford, even now. Even with a steep pay rise and fat bonus coming my way.

One day. One day, every block in this city will be open to me, and men like Lola's Uncle Ray will beg for me to represent them. Maybe I will, maybe I won't. It'll be for me to decide.

I blow out a harsh breath and press Lola's buzzer. She's on the top floor—naturally.

"Hello?" She sounds sleepy, like I caught her napping on the sofa. Is she wearing pajamas? Does she have those pillow creases on her cheek? I check my watch: it's 9pm.

"Hello, Lola."

Her gasp crackles through the bronze grate. Then there's a loud buzz, and I push through to the lobby with a savage grin.

She let me in so quickly. Like she's as eager for this as I am.

I'll reward her for that.

It's dark in here, lit by dim sconces on the wall, and the post boxes lining one wall are made of the same bronze as the buzzer. My feet drum against the tiles, and then I'm pounding up the staircase, my palm sweeping up the banister.

I've never come this far before. There are only four floors, but it feels like an age before I crest the top step. Stars wink through a large glass window in one wall, and an abandoned pink marker lays in one corner. I scoop it up, brushing off the dust. When Lola's door swings open, I hold it out like an offering.

"A casualty of last week, I think."

Lola takes the marker from me, cheeks burning. "I wish you'd forget that."

"Never, darling." Forget the first time I laid eyes on Lola? It'd be easier to forget my own name.

Plus, this way I can tease her, can work that adorable flush onto her cheeks. I follow her inside.

This feels so instinctive. Second nature, like of *course* I'd appear at her door late in the evening. Of course she'd lead me inside, even though she's barefoot with only tiny black shorts and a green tank top covering her up. Lola takes me to a small kitchen with high ceilings and a breakfast bar, and nods at a stool.

"Coffee? Or something stronger?"

No, she's not surprised to see me at all. After all, she practically invited me here earlier. *Well, you know where I live,* she said. Fuck, it's been bouncing around my skull ever since.

"Do you live alone?" I ignore her offer for now. If there's a chance at all of my touching her, I want her clear-headed and enthusiastic. But if there isn't, then yes, I'd like to drink my feelings, please. Lola shrugs one shoulder, wrapping her arms around her waist.

"It's a family apartment. Obviously. My cousins stay here when they have business in the city sometimes, but yes, it's just me right now."

"You don't seem very at home."

Lola smirks, but there's no humor in it. "It's lonely. I'm used to my uncle's estate, with family around me all the time. And before that, even the hospital wards were—" She breaks off abruptly, frowning at the floor. "I, um. Can we forget I said that? I didn't want to tell you about that just yet."

I nod, though my chest aches. She was ill? Why doesn't she want to tell me? Maybe I do want that drink. "Then I didn't hear it."

A relieved breath. "Thanks."

We wait. A clock ticks in another room, and traffic rumbles past down below on the street. And when Lola speaks, she sounds so bitter. "It doesn't matter, does it? You already see me differently. Poor sick little Lola."

She looks tired again. Tired of the world.

"No." I slide off my stool, stalking closer. She shakes her head as I get near, glaring at a spot on my shoulder, and she looks so good in the soft lamplight. Like something from a dream.

"I'm healthy now, okay? Can't that be enough?"

"It is." I take her hips and pull her flush against my body. Grind my cock against her, because sometimes actions speak louder than words. "Does this feel like I'm worried you'll break?"

As fast as her anger came, she softens again, her forehead dropping to rest against my chest. Two arms snake around my waist, and she's rocking against me too. Clenching two fistfuls of my suit jacket and trying to squeeze us impossibly tighter.

She feels it too. This unstoppable draw between us. The primal need to get closer, to swallow each other whole.

"Lola," I groan. Her hair smells so good. "Do you know why I came here?" She shakes her head, still rocking against me. "Little liar."

That earns me a laugh, and I drag my chin over the top of her head, my beard rasping against her pink waves. "I came to lick your pussy, Lola. Would you like that?"

There's a squeak, but she doesn't sound horrified. She rubs her hips harder against me, her hot breaths seeping through my shirt.

"Is that a yes? I need the words, darling."

"Such a lawyer," she huffs. "*Yes.*"

* * *

"Lie back on the bed."

Lola crawls onto the mattress, her hands and knees sinking into the plush white covers. Her tiny shorts cling to her peachy little ass, and I watch it sway with my jaw clenched.

51

"You're so bossy, Julian."

I tilt my head, standing a few feet away. My hands are tucked loosely in my pockets and my shoulders are relaxed, but inside, my heart is pounding. "I thought you liked that." She certainly blushes when she hears me giving orders in the office.

The sheets rustle as Lola makes herself comfortable, and I take a moment to peer around her bedroom. It's a large white room, with one door to an en suite and another to a walk-in closet. Floor-length white drapes cover huge glass windows, and a thick sage green rug covers most of the floorboards. It smells like fresh linen and chamomile.

There's a king sized bed, two nightstands, a laptop glowing on an armchair.

No other signs of life.

You can tell Lola hasn't lived here long purely by the lack of color, and suddenly I'd pay good money to see her *last* bedroom. To see what she hung on the walls, and which vibrant shades she splashed everywhere. To smell her scented candles.

The brightest pop of color in *this* room is her pink hair, splayed over her pillows.

Lola stares at me, eyes bright and lips parting. Her finger draws gentle circles on her stomach. "Are you just gonna stand there?"

I bite out a laugh. "No." My shoes land on the rug, and the bed dips under my weight as I crawl over the mattress. I prowl up the length of Lola's body, until my face hovers above hers and my hands are braced by her shoulders.

She twitches when I brush a kiss to her throat, and I press my question into her heated skin. "Is that how it is? Are you going to be a brat, darling?"

Tentative arms wind around my neck. "It works for Oliver."

A laugh rumbles through my chest into hers, and I sink a little lower. Feel the softness of her body against my hard, unforgiving one. The dips and swells of her curves. "Believe me, Lola, I like you a lot more than I like him."

When I lift my head, she looks so fucking pleased.

God. I'm addicted to this woman. All I've done is crawl on top of her, and already I'm giddy with her. Intoxicated by her heat, her scent, her smile. I kiss her roughly, slanting our mouths together, and it's self-preservation. I need her just as lost to this as I am.

Lola squirms beneath me. She presses her soft tits against my chest; hooks an ankle over my calf. She's rubbing and panting and whimpering for me, and fuck, this is better than any triumph in court.

"Up." I ease back and lift her tank top over her head, tossing it onto the rug and following it with her bra. When Lola flops back against the sheets, her nipples are hard and rosy in the cool bedroom.

I duck my head. Lap at one with my tongue, then the other, and all the while Lola tugs at my hair and moans.

She's so sweet. Like sugar dusts her skin. Her fingers scrabble at my collar, but I shift out of reach.

"No, I think I'll stay dressed tonight, Lola." There's something so pleasing about the image of her sprawled out and naked for me, while I loom over her in a shirt and waistcoat and tie. Something so decadent and depraved. And she gets it, because she blushes even harder and whimpers, then helps me wriggle her shorts and panties down her thighs.

Of course, there are drawbacks to my plan. When I trail kisses down her writhing body, pausing to suck a bruise on her hip bone, when I dip my tongue into her cute belly button, my cock aches from pressing into my fly, and there's no relief.

At least when I lie between her spread thighs, I can rock my hips into the mattress, and though it hurts, it's a good kind of hurt.

Just like my feelings for this girl.

"Lola." Her thigh muscles jump and shudder under my palms. I rub smoothing trails over them, up and down. And there, so close she must feel my heavy breaths, is her slick, swollen pussy. "Lola, darling, you're ever so wet."

It's obvious even without touching her. Her inner thighs are shiny with it, and the air is laden with her sweet, musky scent. A growl rises in my throat and I lunge forward, licking a stripe up her seam.

Lola gasps, hips rocking up to meet my tongue.

"Good girl," I grate out. She whimpers again. "Fuck, you're sweet. Who needs cake pops when I can eat this cunt?"

Her giggles fade into moans. And I'm feverish with her, with her taste and her needy sounds. I lick her until my jaw aches; I slide one then two fingers inside her, pumping them over her sensitive inner walls. I knead her soft tit, pinching and plucking her hard nipple, and every gasp, every cry, is music to my hind brain.

Mine.

Lola is mine. I want to keep her.

"Julian."

She's panting. Hanging onto my hair for dear life, yanking and twisting at the dark strands, and I stop sucking on her clit long enough to tell her, "Don't make me bald, Lola. I don't think you'd like me as much without hair."

A gentle kick to my ass. "I *would.* Oh my god, oh my god—"

I like to pretend that she's praying to me.

Because it's been torture, having her so near in the office and not being able to touch her. Not being able to taste. And sitting in the backseat of that car together, her vanilla scent in my lungs, feeling her warmth *right there* and yet keeping my hands to myself?

Pure torment. I pay some of that torment back now, tenfold.

I draw my spare hand down and gently spank her pussy. I shove her thigh over my shoulder and shove my face deeper, replacing my fingers with my tongue. I *own* her body, inside and out, and when I slide two fingers back inside her, Lola is hoarse with begging.

"Come on, Lola," I coax, fingers pumping in and out, my hips rocking against the bed. "Flood my tongue. Give it up, mi amor." I suck her clit into my mouth one more time and she arches off the bed, stiff and shuddering. Her pussy clamps down on my fingers, waves pulsing through her body, and her breath seizes.

She's so perfect. Fuck, I almost can't stand it.

Lola lets out a strangled cry, then flops back onto the mattress. Sated. Damp with sweat. I extricate myself as gently as I can, drawing my fingers out and sucking them clean, and she's salty and sweet. I'm already hooked on her taste.

Heavy-lidded eyes watch me, lost in a chaotic mound of pillows. "I can't believe you kept your clothes on. You're such a deviant, Julian."

I snort. If only she knew *half* the things I wanted to do with her. But hey—she'll find out in good time.

"I'm your deviant." I crawl up to lay beside her, and my cock is throbbing against my fly, but I don't care. I won't rush her. I won't be the villain everyone thinks I am. A cynical part of me waits for Lola to send me away now that her curiosity has been sated, now that she's successfully hunted the office tiger, but she just rolls over and cuddles into my chest, flicking at my shirt buttons.

Sweet relief.

"I *will* get you naked sometime."

I grin at the ceiling. "Excellent. I look forward to it."

"So you…" Lola's voice is halting. She buries closer into my neck. "You'll want to do that again?"

Ah, I see. We're afraid of the same thing. Of making ourselves vulnerable and only getting one taste before being tossed aside. Forgotten.

That would never happen to Lola. Not with me around, anyway, so I roll over without warning, caging her in my arms. "You are *mine*, Lola Briggs." I nip the tip of her nose, and she giggles, relaxing already. "Of course I want to do that again."

Eight

Lola

I float into the lobby on a cloud. Julian's already here, lounging against the bronze post boxes in a tailored navy suit, and he straightens when he sees me, his dark gaze scorching me as I hop down the last few stairs. His chest expands as he takes in my flippy yellow dress, patterned with daisies.

"Fuck," Julian mutters.

Good. I hoped he'd like it.

He takes my hand as we walk out to the car, and I dart a glance at the front seat, but it's empty. "Oliver finally left you alone with me, huh?"

Julian smirks and opens the rear door wide. "No suitcase today?"

"Nope." The cool leather brushes against my bare legs as I slide in. "I'm getting a bunch of cake pops delivered by a local bakery that I've sent my recipes, and then I'm selling them in a nearby investment firm this afternoon as a trial run. My uncle set it up."

I wait for Julian to say something sarcastic about how Uncle Ray keeps paving the way, but he doesn't. He just smiles at me, eyes crinkling. "Good."

Neither of us point out that I don't really need to be at Irving & Vance today. I could've had the cake pops delivered to my apartment, but then I'd have missed *this*. My morning ride with Julian. Stolen moments with him at the office. I couldn't stay away.

Three more days. It's Wednesday today, and Julian will be done with Lola-sitting by Friday night. My chest throbs.

I hate the thought of not seeing my grumpy lawyer every day.

The car drifts through morning traffic, the driver's window cracked and the radio humming, and I shoot Julian a nervous smile. He frowns, looks like he's about to say something, but then his phone rings. He pulls it out with a muttered curse. "Excuse me, Lola."

This is what it would be like, I guess—our time together. Julian's a busy man. A high-powered lawyer, and that comes with long hours and lots of urgent phone calls. Is that something I want to be around? Uncle Ray was barely home when I was a kid.

I sink back against the seat, mouth twisting.

Reality is such a bitch.

He's still on the phone when we pull up outside the office. I open my own door before he can reach it, hopping out onto the sidewalk. Julian rounds the car, and he gives me a rueful look as we enter the lobby.

He doesn't take my hand again. I guess he can't.

He barks something down the phone. He sounds grumpy.

The elevator doors sweep open, and we crowd in with a few interns and a delivery man. Julian and I stand at the back together, a muffled voice floating out of the phone held to his ear, and as we swoop up the floors, he switches the phone to his other hand.

His knuckles brush mine. My stomach flips.

"No," Julian clips out. "That is unacceptable."

I wrap my whole hand around one of his long fingers, clinging on for dear life, and we ride to the thirty third floor like that, our secret contact hidden behind the wall of interns. When we step out onto our hallway, Julian smiles at me briefly, then tucks his hand in his pocket.

Yeah, no kidding. I'm not gonna paw at him in front of Oliver. The fact that he thinks I would pisses me off, and I stomp after him down the hallway. Jeez. I'm not *that* clueless.

I'm still grouchy an hour later when the cake pops arrive, but the scents of warm sponge and sugary frosting chase all my troubles away. They're spread out in long, flat white boxes, shiny and perfect and bright. Strawberry and vanilla and chocolate and toffee, dipped in chopped nuts or pretty sprinkles.

"Oh, wow," I breathe.

Oliver clatters over to stand at my shoulder. "Holy shit," he says. "Those look legit."

I pluck out a double chocolate cake pop and push the stick into his hand. "Try one. Go on, tell me what you think."

"I already tried the samples," Oliver argues, but he's staring at his chocolate cake pop with pure lust.

"These are fresh, though, and warm, and a proper bakery made them. They used my recipe, but still. It's gonna be way better."

The cake pops even *look* better. Neater and evenly sized. My mouth waters just staring at them.

Oliver sinks his teeth in with a groan. His eyes practically cross, and he holds up his thumb. I beam at him, heart light.

This is gonna work! It *is*. With a lot of help from Oliver and Uncle Ray and even Julian, sure, but it will work. Sprinkletown is go.

"I'll take them right over. I want the finance people to smell them while they're warm."

Oliver leads me to the elevator and presses the button. "You're devious, Lola. Mr Rodriguez had better watch out—he's not the only one with the killer instinct."

* * *

After hours of carrying a heavy box of cake pops up and down a skyscraper, I am *tired*. My arms feel like limp noodles, and my sandals drag against the sidewalk as I make my way back to Irving & Vance. I need a glass of water, a banana and a nap, in that order.

It worked, though. My body may be wrecked by today's work, but my brain is lit up and sparking. I beam as I cross the lobby to the elevator, my dress swishing around my thighs. The last few cake pops shift in the box, scraping over the glossy cardboard, but it's much lighter now.

They *sold*. People loved them. Wow.

It's amazing. The best day ever, and all I want to do is tell Julian about it. I slump against the elevator wall, the floors swooping past, and picture his expression. He'll be so proud.

Oliver's not at his desk when I reach our floor, so I shuffle right past and thump Julian's door with my elbow. He calls out in his low voice, and I fumble the handle down then step inside.

He spins to face me in his chair.

I hold my box up. "Special delivery."

When Julian brightens, I can't believe I was ever afraid of this man. He's a teddy bear masquerading as a scary lawyer, and when he pats his thigh, I kick the door shut and practically skip over, exhaustion forgotten.

I set the box carefully on his desk—no more carpet disasters—then sink onto Julian's lap. He sweeps my hair over one shoulder, pressing kisses to my neck.

"I thought you were desperate for a cake pop."

Julian snorts and wraps a possessive arm around my waist. "I'm desperate for *something*. This dress is cruel, Lola. An act of aggression. You're trying to give me a heart attack at work."

I hum, kicking my heels. "Oliver did say I have killer instinct."

"He's right." Long, elegant fingers gather my dress slowly up my thighs. I puff out a laugh and lean back against his chest, legs inching wider.

Julian doesn't touch me yet, though. He traces maddening circles on my inner thighs, but he murmurs in my ear. "You were annoyed at me this morning. For talking on the phone."

I bite my lip. Busted.

"I'm working on my grumpy reputation so we can match," I say, trying to joke it away. Because it seems so petty now, hours later. So embarrassing.

But Julian squeezes me, not buying it. "Lola. Tell me."

And there's nothing for it except to screw my eyes shut and force out the words. "I just—all I wanted as a little girl was my Uncle Ray's attention. And he was always too busy, taking calls or having meetings or drinking whiskey in his study with other powerful men. Sometimes it felt like he barely even noticed me before I got sick. And I know that I'm not a kid anymore and you don't owe me anything, but I..."

Julian licks my pulse point. "You want my full attention."

I choke out a laugh. It sounds so dumb. "Yeah. I guess so." And I wholly expect him to laugh it off too or even be annoyed, but Julian rumbles with dark satisfaction. Like he *loves* hearing how bad I've got it for him. How possessive I am with every scrap of his time.

"I would like the same."

I splutter, feet swinging. "Yeah?"

"Yes. I'm jealous of your cake pops." Those teasing circles on my thighs creep closer to my center, closer to the pink lace of my panties and the aching, needy part of me behind them. "I won't take them away, of course, because they are important to you. But I would like it stated on the record that I'd prefer to be the center of your world."

I frown at his darkened laptop screen. "Are you making fun of me?"

I can't tell anymore, but Julian growls and nips my earlobe. "No. I'm explaining to you that my work is important and I cannot neglect it, but I understand your frustrations because I feel them too. And I hope we can find a balance together, because if there's one thing you can be sure of, Lola, it's that you are *always* on my mind. Day and night. Here and everywhere else. Okay, mi amor?"

Yes.

Yes, it makes sense, and it's so okay that I can't stop smiling. I flip the cake pop box open and drag it closer. "Which flavor?"

Julian sucks in a ragged breath, burying his face in my hair. "Vanilla, of course."

I lift the last vanilla cake pop out, passing him the stick. It's dipped in white chocolate and covered with pink sprinkles. His dark eyes bore into me as he takes his first bite.

"Delicious," Julian rasps, licking a stray crumb off his bottom lip, and god, I can't take it anymore. His sharp jaw and those cheekbones—that beard and his soulful eyes. I slide off his lap onto the floor, kneeling between his spread legs, half hidden under the shelter of his desk.

Julian watches me tug his belt open with a strained expression, then sets his half-finished cake pop on the desk. "I can't eat while you do this, Lola. It's too much, even for me."

I laugh, his zipper crackling as I tug it down. When I draw out his cock, it's thick and warm in my hand. He's already hard, his shaft pulsing under my fingers when I squeeze it gently, and Julian spreads his legs wider and lounges in his desk chair like a king.

Long fingers spear through my loose hair. "Lick the tip, Lola. Treat it like another cake pop—but watch your teeth." Julian chuckles at his own joke, rolling his neck. "There's my good girl."

Flames lick at my insides, and I shift on my knees. What is it about Julian calling me a good girl that makes me so freaking wet? And he *knows* it too, the bastard, because he's watching me with primal satisfaction etched on his handsome face.

Last night, he buried his face in my pussy like he wanted to drown in there, and I try to bring the same fervor now. I work the base of his cock with my hands, gripping and twisting, and run my tongue over every bare inch of skin.

I rain kisses over him.

I suckle on the tip.

I slurp him all the way down, as far as my throat will allow.

"Yes," Julian hisses, the chair squeaking as his hips buck. "Fuck,

Lola. Your mouth. Your pretty mouth."

I hum, and I'm rewarded with a ragged groan. He strokes my hair and pulls on the strands; he scratches my scalp and rubs my earlobes between finger and thumb. Julian can't stop *touching* me, his cock thrusting carefully past my lips, and I can smell him. He's soap and salt and fine cologne. A faint undercurrent of musk. Freaking delicious. And he's hot, too, his cock so hot under my hands, his thighs bracketing me with firm warmth, and I've never felt so surrounded.

"Look at you." Each word grinds out of his chest. "Look at you taking me so deep. The *sounds* you make, Lola."

I hum again, and he thrusts harder. Hits the back of my throat and makes my eyes tear, but I moan loudly. I want him losing control; I *like* him coming undone.

"Lola, my Lola."

We're so lost in Julian's muttered curses and my moans and the creaking chair that we don't hear the office door open. We don't hear anything, until my Uncle Ray bellows and charges across the office. "Lola-Rose! Get *off* her."

He drags me out from under the desk by the elbow, and Julian jerks back and stuffs his cock away. I bang my knee on the table leg as I emerge, pain radiating through the bone.

By the doorway, the two old lawyers from the top floor crowd inside with a white-faced Oliver.

"Uncle Ray!" I yank my arm free, cheeks burning and eyes damp. Of *course* this would happen during my first blow job—I'd have an accidental audience of judgy old men. Fuck my life. "You should've knocked!"

My uncle gapes at me, turning crimson to his thinning gray hair. "This is an office," he bellows. "These people are at work, Lola. *You* might be playing make-believe at having a job, but that asshole knows better!" He jabs a finger at Julian over my shoulder, but my ears are ringing. My chest feels raw.

That's what he thinks I'm doing. Playing make-believe.

…Is he right?

I wrap my arms around my waist, face numb.

"Don't speak to her like that," Julian's saying somewhere behind me, his voice muffled. Uncle Ray yells something in return, but I don't hear it. I don't hear any of it.

"It's not Julian's fault," I rasp. "I—I came on to him."

"He knows better."

"He's right," Julian snarls. "I should've known to lock the fucking door."

The older lawyers are arguing now too. Everyone's yelling except Oliver, who stares at me with shock and pity. He jerks his chin at the doorway, and I stumble forward, relieved.

It's cool in our—his office. Somehow I don't think I'll be invited back. And it's quiet, except for the muffled yelling and the *click* as Oliver picks up his desk phone.

"They're hypocrites," he mutters, stabbing at the buttons as he dials. "Show me any powerful man in this city and I'll show you someone who's hooked up in his office. I'll bet half your cousins were conceived on a desk—no offense, Lola. Don't let them get to you. You're right, they should have knocked."

I still feel so ashamed.

"Will Julian be fired?"

Oliver says nothing, holding the phone to his ear. Then: "Yes, right away please. Back to her apartment."

Guess there's my answer. The phone settles back in the cradle with a click, and my heart sinks down to the floor.

"The car will be waiting for you. Want me to take you home?"

I shake my head. I've caused so much trouble already, but

maybe Oliver sees how I'm holding on by a thread, because he huffs and grabs his jacket.

"Screw it. I'm not going to listen to them yelling at each other. Bunch of babies."

Julian's not a baby. He stood up for me in there, and now he's going to get fired, and what have I done? Run away like a coward. I hover, staring at the door, until Oliver takes my elbow.

"Come on, Lola. You can't help Julian now. Let's get out of here."

* * *

Maybe I can't help Julian, but I can send a damn text. I write it in the back seat of the car, typing angrily and then deleting it all again, trying to figure out the right thing to say. The words that could help Julian.

When I finally press send, a weight lifts off my shoulders.

Uncle Ray. I know you're upset by what you saw, but I'm not happy with you either. We shouldn't have done that in the office, you're right, but you shouldn't have yelled and treated me like a child. You said a lot of cruel things, and you were very rude to the man I love. I hope you didn't get Julian fired, because that's the man I'll marry one day. Remember that you're dealing with your future nephew-in-law.

Maybe it's presumptuous to think Julian will want anything more to do with me, and he's definitely never suggested he'd marry me, but Uncle Ray doesn't know that. He doesn't know we haven't said the L-word, and it's the best protection I can offer Julian right now. I show Oliver and he nods, jaw tight.

"You tried your best, honey."

Lola

I'm not so sure.

Nine

Julian

W ell, I was supposed to make partner in three months. Instead I'm packing up my office, tossing my belongings into a cardboard box while the sunset scorches the city behind me. Vance and Irving didn't even fire me, the spineless idiots, they just withdrew the promotion. It's clear now that I'll *never* make partner in this firm.

Assholes. As if I'd stay here, whipped and tamed. And as if I haven't caught them doing far worse in their own offices. They're covering their asses, trying to keep Ray Briggs happy.

"What will you do?" Oliver leans against my office wall, watching me pack up. "Apply to other firms?"

I grunt. That's the obvious option, but I don't know if I have it in me to bow and scrape to another set of fools. "Maybe. Or maybe I'll set up my own firm." Lord knows I've got the contacts by now. Most of Irving & Vance's clients request me by name.

Oliver brightens. "Will you take me with you?"

I glance at him, but he's serious. Huh. Well, that's something. "I'll need some time to set up. A few weeks, maybe a month before I can start paying you."

Oliver beams, bouncing over to my desk, and fuck, that enthusiasm is just like Lola. My gut twists. "Okay, I'll wait here for a few weeks. Don't leave me behind, though."

"I won't."

She left *me* behind today, but I know that's a petty thing to think. Who can blame her? Her uncle broke her heart right in front of our eyes, and then we were all too busy yelling and dick-measuring to see her slip out. What was she supposed to do, force a bunch of angry, old-fashioned men to take her seriously after seeing that? They made their minds up about her as soon as they stepped into the office.

Of course, they still take *me* seriously, even her uncle. Hypocrites, the lot of them.

I suspect Oliver had something to do with Lola's escape, but I haven't asked. I don't mind. I'm grateful.

"She sent a text to her uncle," he says suddenly. "Told him to be careful, because he's dealing with his future nephew-in-law."

I snort, heart lifting. She was only trying to protect me, obviously, but for a warm moment I can pretend it's true.

Maybe Lola *could* love me—even after this shit show.

Maybe I could marry her one day.

"Mr Rodriguez?" I grunt, dropping an armful of files in the box. Oliver inches closer. "You'll go and see her, right? I really think she needs you."

Lola needs me? I pause, a stapler in one hand.

I've kept my distance all afternoon. Didn't pester her with calls or rush over to her apartment. I didn't think she'd want to see me at all; didn't think she'd want the reminder. I mean, it's not like she said goodbye or left me a note. She just *disappeared*. Vanished into the air like smoke.

But if she does need me... if she's been waiting for me all these hours...

I drop the stapler with a clatter. "I'll pack up the rest tomorrow."

Oliver grins, herding me back through the door. "Tell her you love her!"

"Stay out of it, Oliver."

"And bring her flowers! Or—no—cake pops!"

I stride down the hallway and jab the elevator button, heart racing. "You watch too much TV. I'm serious. It's not a good look."

Oliver cackles all the way back to his desk. The doors swish apart, and I step into the elevator, swallowing hard.

Enough bad shit for today. I'm going to find my girl.

* * *

Lola doesn't answer the first buzz. I hover on the sidewalk, throat tight, and buzz again, speaking into the grate in case she can hear me. "Lola? It's me. Ah, Julian. Will you let me in, please?"

There's a deathly long pause. My hopes rise and die, one by one, in this pause. Goodbye, hopes.

Then there's a *click* and I shove the door open, heart pounding.

A chance. That's all I need. One chance with her.

I need to make this right.

My shoes smack against the tiles, then I take the stairs three at a time. By the time I reach Lola's floor, there's a stitch in my side and my shirt sticks to my back. I did not think this through. And I can't even recover, because her door opens and then she's watching me. Leaning in the doorway with her arms folded. Dressed in blue silk pajama bottoms and a white camisole.

"Lola," I wheeze. I can't fucking speak, my chest heaving as I catch my breath. "Shit. Sorry. I ran."

Her mouth twitches, but she frowns as I thrust my gift in her direction. I came here via a late night bakery, and they were happy to arrange the cake pops like a bouquet of flowers. Pink and white and lemon yellow cake pops, all round and sweet and covered in sprinkles.

Is this dumb? It feels dumb.

Lola takes the bunch of cake pops from me gingerly, clearing her throat.

"It was Oliver's idea," I say quickly, throwing my assistant under the bus. "He said you needed me."

Lola hums, and she won't meet my eye. I straighten and move closer, finally recovering from my sprint up the stairs, and her chin wobbles when I tip it up so she'll look at me.

"Do you want me here, Lola? Or should I leave? I can't blame you after what happened today, but I've been—I'm—even a few *hours* without you have been torture."

Lola sighs, then takes my wrist and pulls me inside. I follow her lead, though I can't read her at all. Where is my chatty girl? Her slumped shoulders make my stomach churn.

"I'm so sorry, Lola," I tell her once we reach the kitchen. She turns to face me, pale and silent. "They were right. I never should have put you in that position. You are very precious to me, and I let that happen. It's the worst thing I've ever done."

It's true. It's all true. I've been kicking myself all afternoon, dragging myself over hot coals. Do I seriously think I deserve this girl after all that?

Lola scoffs. "You're a lawyer, Julian. I doubt that."

My mouth twitches, but she's not smiling yet, so neither can I. "Oliver told me you texted your uncle."

Her head tilts. "Did it work?"

Ah. Well. No, not really, and at my silence, she folds in on herself. "I'm not fired," I say quickly, "but I can't work there anymore either. Not if I want a real career. Please don't worry about it," I add, because her eyes are damp, and *fuck*, I hate seeing Lola cry. "I'm going to start my own firm. Oliver's coming with me."

A watery smile. Thank god. "You sure you want to hire that brat?"

At last. I'll take every scrap of humor from her, every sign that she's okay. "Yeah, I guess so. Even though he told me to bring you those stupid cake pops." I wave at where Lola set them on the counter, and this time when she looks at them, her expression softens.

"Don't be mad, but I'm kind of sick of cake pops right now. And sick of... playing make-believe."

Fuck. Her uncle is the worst. I cross to Lola and take her by the shoulders, then give her a gentle shake. "Don't listen to that for a second. What you built is real, Lola. You sold all those cake pops today, didn't you?"

She nods, chewing her lip. I swoop down and kiss it until she sighs, melting against my chest. Her hands tangle in my shirt. "Maybe I will keep going with Sprinkletown. But without all the help and favors this time. Just me, figuring it out."

I squeeze her, so proud. "You'll be great. And it will mean more that way."

"Yeah."

72

For a long while, we stand there in silence. Leaning against each other for support, her soft bits pressing against my hard body.

"That was my first blow job," Lola whispers after a while, and she sounds so sad. So mortified. I rest my chin on her head, holding on tight.

"It was so good, my Lola. Forget the way it ended. We'll rewrite it this second, and say it ended as it should have—with me spilling down your pretty throat. We'll say you sucked the life out of me, and then you licked me clean with your kitten tongue. Then I spread you out on my desk and returned the favor."

She pokes my rib. "Maybe I would have spit. You don't know, Julian."

I tut, shaking my head. "Onto my clean carpet? Lola, we talked about this."

Her laughter is a balm to my tired soul. And when she takes my hand, dragging me to her bedroom, I send up a silent prayer of thanks.

She's okay. *We're* okay.

Everything else is mere details.

* * *

"I haven't done this before." Lola's lying flat on her back, naked and flushed, one palm braced on my abs like I might dive on her and ravish her at any moment. She's not wrong, especially since she took such delicious care in peeling off my clothes. "So you'll have to be gentle."

I lean over her, offended. "I'm always gentle. Was I rough with you just now, when you came all over my chin?" I bend down

73

and wipe my beard on her shoulder, demonstrating exactly how much she liked it, and Lola kicks and squirms, her laughter floating up to the ceiling.

"Stop it! God. You're such a jerk." But she's grinning, pulling me closer.

Now, that won't do. I'm a lawyer to my core. "When you say 'stop', mi amor, do you mean I should climb off?"

Lola huffs. "We're not in court right now, Julian." She hooks one leg around my hip, trying to guide me down, but I resist her.

"Indulge me."

By Lola's long sigh, you'd think I was the most tiresome man on Earth. "Okay, no, you infuriating man, I don't want you to stop. I want you to f—fuck me."

Hearing her stumble over that word makes my cock twitch and my chest ache. I brush stray pink strands of hair off her forehead. "Tonight, Lola? You're sure? We can wait, you know. According to your text, we have the rest of our lives—"

She lunges up with a growl, silencing me with her mouth on mine.

She thinks I'm teasing. And maybe I am a little, but I mean it too. As far as I'm concerned, this is my future wife, and I'll wait as long as she needs.

I think, though, if I delay any longer, Lola will scream at the ceiling, so I reach between us and position my cock at her center.

I go slowly, like she said. Gentle and sweet. Nudging inside her, inch by inch, feeling her tight channel stretch around me. A few times, Lola whimpers, and I pause. Wait for her hips to roll again and for her nails to claw my back before I press deeper.

Fuck. She's scorching hot and so wet. Gripping me, *squeezing* me.

"Lola," I rasp, licking at her throat. Nipping her earlobe. "Fuck. You feel like heaven on Earth. You were built for me, sweet girl. Do you like my cock pushing inside you?"

She moans in answer, her nails digging into my shoulders. Her hips rock up, and I slide deeper. *Deeper.*

Yeah. I like it too.

"Good thing they didn't walk in on *this*," I say, and she scoffs and smacks my side. My laugh vibrates through both of us, and fuck, I've never felt this close. So connected, so intimate. So at home.

When our bodies seal flush, we let out twin groans.

I'm sweaty. She's flushed. My arms shake where they're braced at her shoulders, and I can still taste her pussy on my lips. It's messy and awkward but perfect, too, and once we find our rhythm...

I see stars.

"*Shit*, Lola." My hips slam into hers, pounding her up the bed, and she clings to my damp neck. Arches her back and moans. "Do you have any idea how perfect you feel? Such a good girl. Such a—"

She surges up, flipping me onto my back. I grin, chest heaving, as she scrambles up to straddle me, swinging a thigh over my hips.

She's got me. I'm conquered.

Ten

Lola

"Yes, my love. Sit on my cock. Just like that." Julian hisses as I lower down, taking him inside me again, and I grin as I start to move. It takes a second to get my knees in a good position, then we're off, my hips rocking and ass bouncing.

"You're so freaking *chatty*. I did not see that coming. You've got that silent, broody lawyer thing going usually."

I love it, though. There's no room to wonder whether he's having a good time, because Julian sings my filthy praises, loud and clear. And it's a relief, because this feels so freaking good to me too. Like toe-curling, heart-pounding, make-your-hair-stand-on-end good.

The wet noises between our bodies as our flesh slams together... they're obscene. And he's so thick and hard, sliding in and out of my pussy, and the air is heavy with the smell of sex. My inner thighs are pink from Julian's beard rubbing me there, and my clit still tingles from being sucked until I came.

It's wild. I feel like I should be more ashamed, more shy about this, but I'm not. Even after the disaster in his office, how could I be self-conscious when Julian stares up at me like that? Dark-eyed and hungry? Praising me, so reverent.

"Fuck," he says, licking his bottom lip. "Look at your titties bounce."

See? I snatch his hands off my thighs and put them on my tits instead, and Julian growls in approval. He's all too happy to pinch my nipples until my clit throbs. Then he pushes to sit upright, and the new angle makes my breath seize.

He's *everywhere*. Pressing against my clit from behind; his dark belly hairs tickling it from the front. I scrape my nails over the ridges of his abs, and he chokes out a laugh, tensing. "You're a demon, my love."

I start to roll my hips again, not bouncing up and down, but grinding on him. God, that feels perfect, and pleasure floods my body like a shower of warm sparks.

"You're going to come on my cock, Lola." He sounds so freaking confident. So arrogant, and it should not be sexy, but here we are. I loop my arms around his neck, nodding in a daze, and Julian nips my chin. "You feel that? It's the only cock you'll ever need. You're *mine*, Lola Briggs, and I'm going to fuck you every day until you admit it."

I mean, I already know I'm his, but if that's the threat... I could take a few weeks before I tell Julian.

Because this is the best thing I've ever felt. I'm so alive. So grounded in my body, but flying at the same time.

And it's different from when I came on his tongue. This time it's slower and deeper, rolling over me like thunder, and I can't do anything except cling to Julian's shoulders and hold on for dear life. I buck and whimper. I shake and moan. And his long, satisfied sigh—it almost sends me over the edge a second time.

"*Yes*, Lola." He bucks up into me, quick and hard, then warmth blooms between us, and that feels so good too. "*Fuck*."

I slump in his arms, sweaty and sticky and breathless.

It's so perfect. Then my stomach growls.

Julian chuckles, tracing his fingertips up and down my spine. "Guess you're hungry for a cake pop after all."

* * *

Four years later

My husband's office is my favorite delivery. Sprinkletown has dozens of workers these days selling cake pops in skyscrapers through the city, but I always take this building. Maybe I'm the jealous type—but more likely, I need my Julian fix. After all, it's been *hours* since he woke me up with his face between my legs.

I cross the lobby, a large box of cake pops balanced in my arms. I'll start on the lower floors and work my way up.

Julian's firm is in a smaller building than Irving & Vance, but personally, I think it's nicer. The rooms are brighter, with big windows and art deco tiles on the ground floor, then polished floorboards above. *No carpet,* Julian told me once with a smirk. Whatever. There are still some rugs I can aim for.

There are fewer lawyers working here too, but the ones Julian has are the best. Killers, Oliver calls them, draping himself over the copy machine to flirt with the older women.

I don't care if they're vicious. They're all suckers for my cake pops, so that works for me.

When I first brought a delivery here, Julian asked if I wanted him to tell them all I was his girlfriend. I told him no. I'd had enough 'favors' from my Uncle Ray, and I wanted to do things properly this time. Julian just smiled at me. God, it makes me so gooey when he's proud.

And they bought so many cake pops. Julian was right—it felt even better since I did it myself.

Of course, *now* they recognize me. The firm is four years old, and I've been Julian's wife for three. A few jump up when they see me coming toward their desks, but I don't think they feel pressured to buy my cake pops. Mostly, they're worried about my swollen belly.

I save the best for last. The sexy grump himself. Oliver whistles when I walk past his desk, half empty cake pop box held aloft, and he waves a hand at my stomach. "You have a license to drive that thing?"

Yeah, twins look ridiculous on me. "Shut up, Oliver," I tell him sweetly, then pause with the box. "Double chocolate cake pop?"

A minute later, Julian lurches up behind his desk when he sees me too. He rounds it quickly, then crosses to take the box off me and spreads a hand over my stomach. "I wish you'd make Oliver do your dirty work."

"I don't think that's in his contract."

Julian grunts, sliding one hand around to rub circles on my lower back. "One of your own minions, then."

Yeah. I *am* tired. Maybe I'll stop now until the babies are born—especially if it smooths that worried pinch to my husband's forehead. I reach out and smooth it with my thumb. "You fuss too much."

Julian leads me to his chair, expression sour. It creaks like crazy when I sit down, and my sore feet tingle with relief. "I fuss the exact right amount, thank you."

"So *grumpy*."

Julian smirks, then sinks to his knees in front of the chair. He backs up until he's half hidden under the desk, eyes sparkling with mischief. "Did you lock the door?"

I bite my lip. "No. Did you?"

Julian shakes his head, flipping my skirt up my thighs. "Oh, dear. Will we never learn?"

He's teasing. Oliver knows better than to come in here without knocking, and besides–what's Julian going to do? Fire himself?

"I bet you're an absolute tyrant of a boss."

Julian hums, rubbing his cheek on my thigh, and he doesn't deny it. "Lola, my love, I learned it all from you."

Ha. Well he said it, not me. "Come on, minion," I tease, grabbing a handful of his hair. "Get back to work."

* * *

Thanks for reading Sweet Tooth! I hope you liked it :)

For more NSFW office antics, check out Filthy Headlines. *My gorgeous new boss doesn't trust me. Guess he's right—I'm an undercover reporter.*

And for a bonus instalove story, grab your copy of Beauty & The Kingpin. *I'm a florist. He's the king of the underworld.*

Happy reading!

Cassie xxx

Teaser: Thief

There is someone in my home. *There is someone in my fucking home.* The thought rattles around my foggy brain, dragging me out of sleep; it pounds in my blood with every anxious squeeze of my heart. I know something is wrong the second I wake up with my face mashed into the pillows and the hairs raised on the back of my neck. My jaw is clenched and my muscles are tensed ready for a fight, and my back is damp with sweat.

I can't hear them yet. Can't hear anything but the shallow rasp of my own breath and the frantic *thud, thud, thud* of my heart.

But I know it—the same way you know there's someone nearby, even when they're not making a sound. *Especially* when they're not making a sound. It's the telltale, horrifying absence of noise.

Then my microwave gives a loud ping, and I choke back a panicked laugh. Some fucking burglar.

It's dark in here, the bed sheets tangled around my legs, and I snatch my glasses off my nightstand, nearly jabbing my own eye in my rush to get them on. The weight of my cell phone is reassuring in my palm, my thumb blurring over the screen as I dial 911.

I'm not charging out there like Rambo. I'm not a small man, but I wrestle code, not intruders, and only an idiot risks facing down a gun for the sake of their ego.

The operator is calm. Almost bored-sounding as she reels off a list of standard questions, including whether I have a roommate or a girlfriend or neighbors with thin walls. Basically, she's asking: *am I sure I'm not a dumbass?*

But this is the penthouse apartment. The only thing that ever knocks on my walls is the rough winds, storming high above the city. Still, I answer her questions in a hushed voice, straining for more sounds beyond my bedroom door.

There's nothing. For a horrible moment I think maybe I dreamed it, and I'll have to explain to a bunch of grumpy cops that I'm scared of things that go bump in the night. But then a sharp noise shatters the quiet: the unmistakable clatter of a fork dropped in my kitchen sink, and my muscles all tense rock hard again.

The burglar is *eating?* What the fuck?

"The police will be with you in eight minutes, Mr Arnoult," the operator says, with no hint that she recognizes my name. Good. That's one less thing for my lawyer to worry about. I thank her and hang up, even as she invites me to stay on the line, and toss my phone to the mattress.

Eight minutes.

Eight long minutes.

A lot could happen in eight minutes.

***

I fully expect the burglar to ransack my apartment. To tear the valuable paintings off the walls and go through my electronics; maybe steal my laptop or copy my hard drive. I *definitely* expect them to go hunting for that damn sapphire I couldn't resist, but I still yelp in shock when they burst into my bedroom.

It's stupid, really. According to my schedule and everyone who knows my movements, I shouldn't be here tonight. The burglar clearly thinks they're alone since they ate my damn food, so why wouldn't they charge around like they own the place?

But there's nothing in my bedroom except *me,* my eyes wide and my hair rumpled and my hands raised in the universal signal of surrender. My burglar sucks in a shocked breath, slamming to a halt in the doorway, then tilts her head to the side.

Her head. Yeah. Because there's no mistaking that slender silhouette, framed by the light from my living room.

My burglar is a woman.

"Uh," I say, scanning her toned body for weapons, her lithe limbs dressed all in black. There's no gun, no glint of a blade, and apparently relief makes me even dumber than before, because I blurt, "Can I help you?"

She puffs out a laugh. She sounds winded, too, like this is too awful to believe. Well, fuck that. She's the one who broke in here, and my voice is harsh when I grind out, "The police are on their way."

Still no movement. No rush for the door.

Slowly, trying not to spook her, I switch on my bedside lamp–and it's my turn to lose all my air.

Because she's beautiful. Even in that ugly black beanie, she's so pretty she's hard to look at. With her creamy skin and pink mouth and the tiny black mole on her upper lip, it's like staring directly into the sun. And when she sighs and tugs the hat off, caramel waves tumbling around her shoulders, I forget how to swallow.

My shoulder blades press against the headboard. I tug the bed covers over my lap.

"I was thinking about teaching yoga in prison earlier," my burglar tells me, casually wandering into my bedroom like we really are roommates. "I jinxed it. Such a rookie error." She wanders to the window, pulling back the dark drapes to stare at the streets below, and she doesn't seem stressed. Just lost in her own thoughts.

"I'm sorry," I rasp, though fuck knows why I'm commiserating with her. "I do that sometimes with important meetings. I picture myself screwing it all up, and then I play it out exactly the same way. Like I wrote myself a script."

She smiles at me, clearly charmed, and lets the curtain drop. "Not many powerful men would admit that, Spencer Arnoult."

I shrug one shoulder, not sure what to say. I don't like many powerful men, even though theoretically they're my peers. They're too concerned with hurting people to prove they can–like little boys frying ants under a magnifying glass. I've been that ant. I *won't* be that man. "How do you–"

I cut myself off with an irritated grunt. *How do you know my name?* That's what I was about to ask, like she's a girl I bumped into at a party or a bar like a normal person. But of course she knows my fucking name. She's here to burgle me. She probably knows every single thing about me–everything worth stealing, anyway.

"Aren't you going to run?" I ask her instead, and my beautiful thief shakes her head, her golden hair shifting against those shoulders.

Those *shoulders*. Those arms, those legs, Jesus Christ. I didn't know I liked sculpted muscles on women until I met my burglar, and now I'm mentally subscribing to Sports Illustrated even as I can't tear my eyes away from her. She looks like she wandered off the Olympics gymnastics team.

"There's no point. I didn't plan for a quick escape, you know? I thought I'd have hours to get around your security system and work my way down to the lobby. The fact is, Spencer," she flops onto the edge of my bed, kicking out her legs and crossing her ankles, "I've screwed up. I'll go down with dignity."

I stare at her feet. "You're not wearing any shoes."

She wiggles her toes in those black socks. "Nope. Wouldn't have been comfy in the suitcase."

"In the–" I break off, pinching the bridge of my nose. I got a load of old cases delivered from storage this morning, but that was *hours* ago, and the delivery men were not exactly gentle. She was in there that whole time? Is she dehydrated?

I prod at my phone, checking the time on the screen. Four minutes until the cops arrive. "You really should run," I tell her. "I'll help you past the security system, but you're on your own from there."

I don't examine why I so desperately want to help her. Why I *need* to get her out of here before a bunch of pushy, forceful police barge in here and grab her, push her around, shout at her and put her slender wrists in handcuffs—

"Spencer." Her soft voice cuts through my rising stress, and a small, gloved hand slips into mine. "Don't worry, okay? I got caught, fair and square, and I knew the risks. You shouldn't feel guilty."

This is the weirdest conversation of my life.

But it only gets stranger as she lets out a huff, collapsing back on the bed and resting her head on my thigh. I stare at her for what feels like an eternity, then smooth a cautious palm over her hair. It feels like warm silk.

My burglar hums. She squirms closer, her hand still in mine.

When was the last time I touched someone like this? When was the last time *I* was touched–with affection and intimacy and no underlying motives? I don't remember.

I really don't remember, and now that I've had this tiny taste, my body is screaming for more. My chest aches and my skin flushes and I want ten more minutes with her holding my hand. Ten more minutes, and I'd trade anything. She can take the stupid sapphire. *Anything.*

"Please run," I grit out. "Please. I wish I never called them. I thought–I thought you were some asshole with a gun."

She nods, squeezing my fingers. "You did the right thing. That would have been dangerous."

God. I swallow hard, and my throat is tight. Outside, in the street far below, faint sirens approach the building.

"Please…"

"Tabitha," she supplies. Her pink lips curve into a smile as she watches me, staring like she's as fascinated by this connection as I am.

I grip her hand tighter, willing her to listen to me, damn it. "Please, Tabitha. I'm begging you. Go."

"Nope." She pops the 'p', and I huff and bend forward, my forehead touching hers.

"They might be rough with you." I can barely say the words.

But: "I'll handle it," she murmurs, and *no.* I can't be part of this. I won't allow it–won't let her get hurt on my behalf. I don't care what she's done, don't care what laws she's broken.

When a fist pounds on my apartment door, I'm already resolved.

"Wait here," I tell her, brushing a kiss on her forehead, my face hot as I straighten, nudging her up so I can climb out of bed. "I mean it. Don't go anywhere."

Her soft laugh follows me out of the room. "Jeez, Spencer. Make up your mind."

* * *

Check out Thief!

xxx

Cassie Mint

About the Author

Cassie writes outrageous, OTT instalove with tons of sugar and spice. She loves cookie dough, summer barbecues, and her gorgeous cat Missy.

You can connect with me on:

🌐 https://www.authorcassiemint.com

📘 https://www.facebook.com/cassiemintauthor

🔗 https://www.bookbub.com/authors/cassie-mint

🔗 https://www.amazon.com/~/e/B08VF8BPWG

Subscribe to my newsletter:

✉ https://www.authorcassiemint.com/newsletter